THIS BOOK BELONGS TO

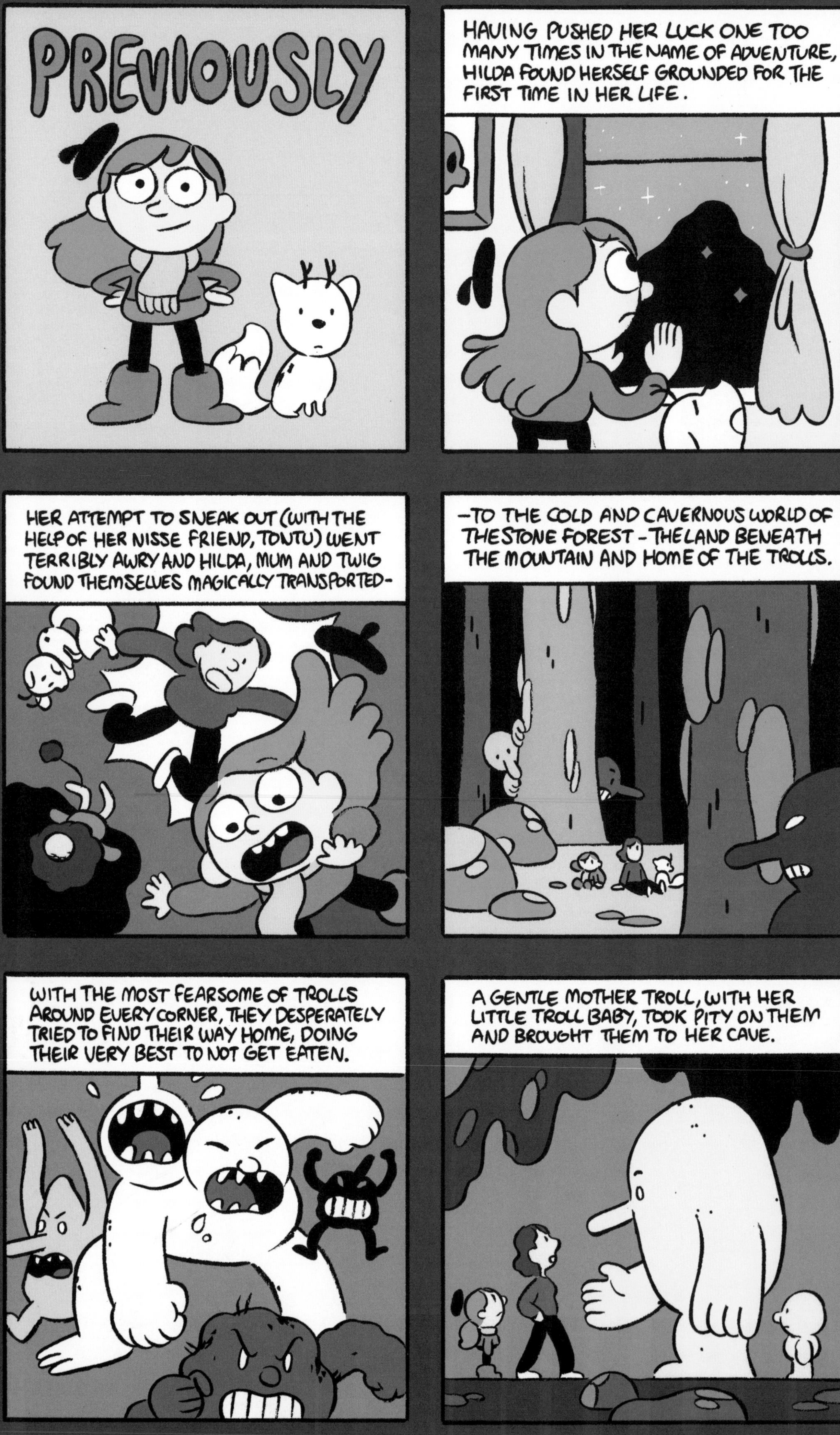
PREVIOUSLY
HAVING PUSHED HER LUCK ONE TOO MANY TIMES IN THE NAME OF ADVENTURE, HILDA FOUND HERSELF GROUNDED FOR THE FIRST TIME IN HER LIFE.
HER ATTEMPT TO SNEAK OUT (WITH THE HELP OF HER NISSE FRIEND, TONTU) WENT TERRIBLY AWRY AND HILDA, MUM AND TWIG FOUND THEMSELVES MAGICALLY TRANSPORTED-
-TO THE COLD AND CAVERNOUS WORLD OF THE STONE FOREST - THE LAND BENEATH THE MOUNTAIN AND HOME OF THE TROLLS.
WITH THE MOST FEARSOME OF TROLLS AROUND EVERY CORNER, THEY DESPERATELY TRIED TO FIND THEIR WAY HOME, DOING THEIR VERY BEST TO NOT GET EATEN.
A GENTLE MOTHER TROLL, WITH HER LITTLE TROLL BABY, TOOK PITY ON THEM AND BROUGHT THEM TO HER CAVE.

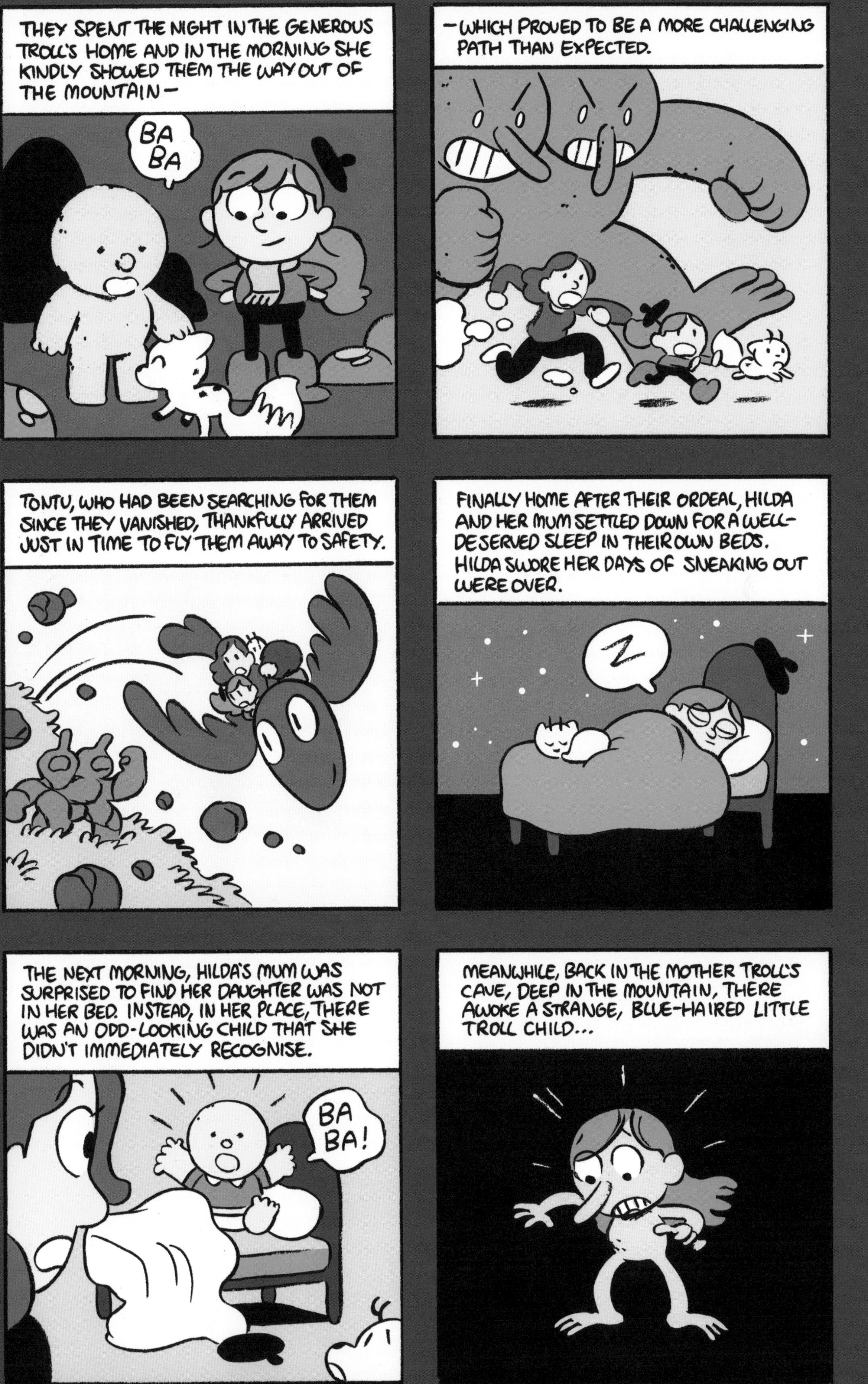
THEY SPENT THE NIGHT IN THE GENEROUS TROLL'S HOME AND IN THE MORNING SHE KINDLY SHOWED THEM THE WAY OUT OF THE MOUNTAIN–
BA BA
–WHICH PROVED TO BE A MORE CHALLENGING PATH THAN EXPECTED.
TONTU, WHO HAD BEEN SEARCHING FOR THEM SINCE THEY VANISHED, THANKFULLY ARRIVED JUST IN TIME TO FLY THEM AWAY TO SAFETY.
FINALLY HOME AFTER THEIR ORDEAL, HILDA AND HER MUM SETTLED DOWN FOR A WELL-DESERVED SLEEP IN THEIR OWN BEDS. HILDA SWORE HER DAYS OF SNEAKING OUT WERE OVER.
Z
THE NEXT MORNING, HILDA'S MUM WAS SURPRISED TO FIND HER DAUGHTER WAS NOT IN HER BED. INSTEAD, IN HER PLACE, THERE WAS AN ODD-LOOKING CHILD THAT SHE DIDN'T IMMEDIATELY RECOGNISE.
BA BA!
MEANWHILE, BACK IN THE MOTHER TROLL'S CAVE, DEEP IN THE MOUNTAIN, THERE AWOKE A STRANGE, BLUE-HAIRED LITTLE TROLL CHILD...

FOR PHILIPPA AND ROBIN.

SPECIAL THANKS TO PHILIPPA RICE, ROBIN PEARSON, SAM ARTHUR, STEPHANIE SIMPSON, KURT MUELLER, HOLLY DYER, FION FITZGERALD, JON MCNAUGHT, BRYAN KORN, EVERYBODY AT FLYING EYE, SILVERGATE AND MERCURY FILMWORKS; AND TO MUM, DAD AND AMELIA FOR THEIR PATIENCE AND SUPPORT.

FIRST EDITION PUBLISHED IN 2019 BY FLYING EYE BOOKS,
AN IMPRINT OF NOBROW LTD. 27 WESTGATE STREET, LONDON, E8 3RL.

1 3 5 7 9 10 8 6 4 2

PUBLISHED IN THE US BY NOBROW (US) INC.
PRINTED IN LATVIA ON FSC® CERTIFIED PAPER

MIX
Paper from responsible sources
FSC® C002795

ISBN 978-1-911171-17-1
WWW.FLYINGEYEBOOKS.COM

HILDA
AND THE
MOUNTAIN
KING

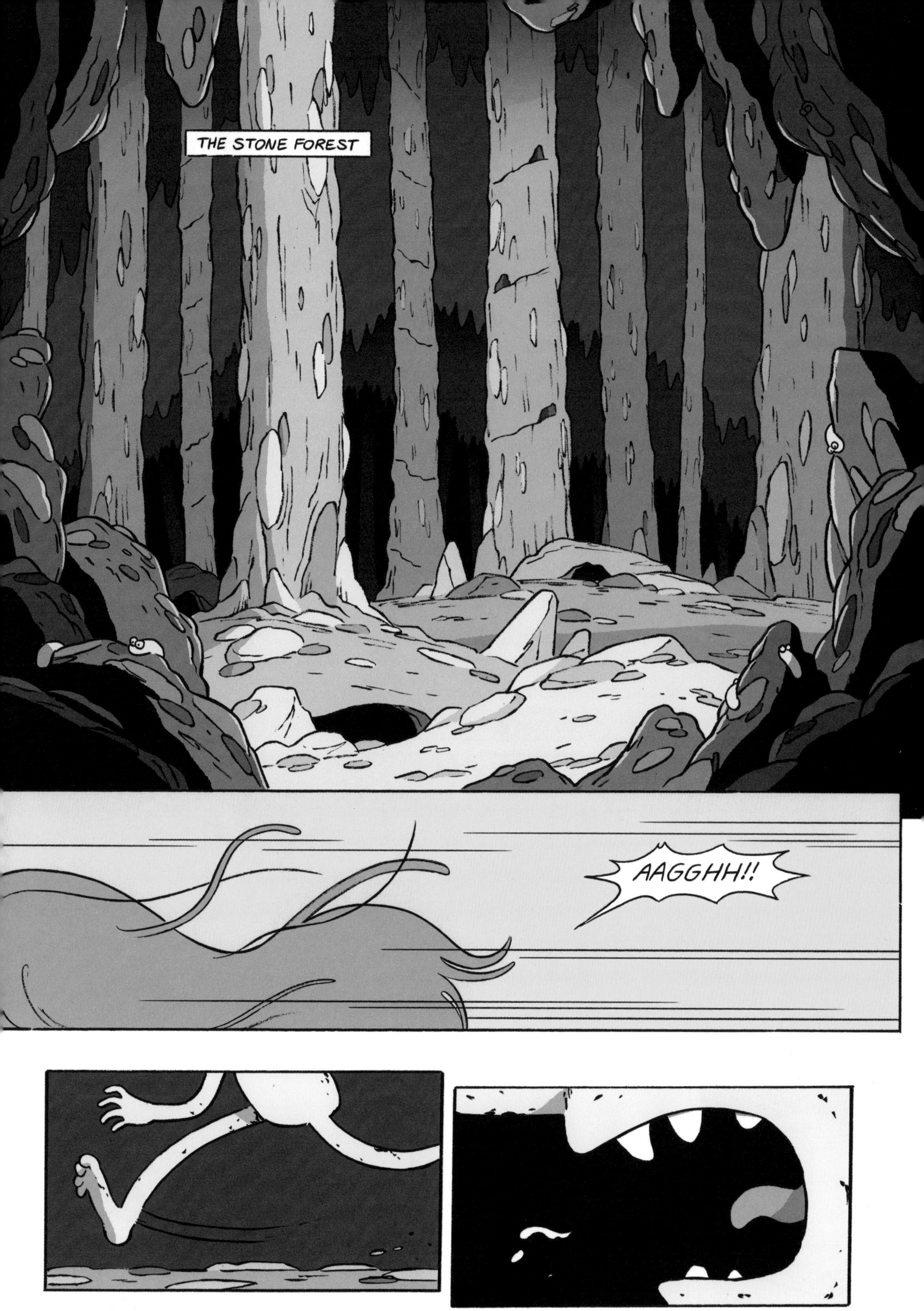
THE STONE FOREST
AAGGHH!!

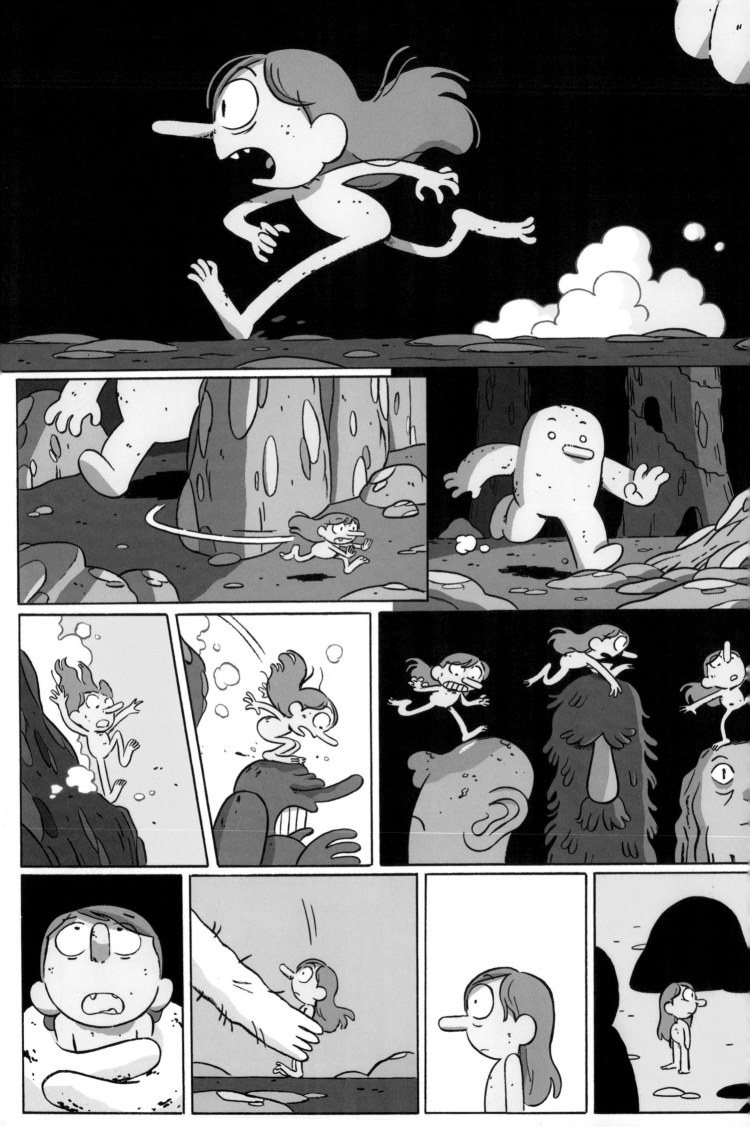

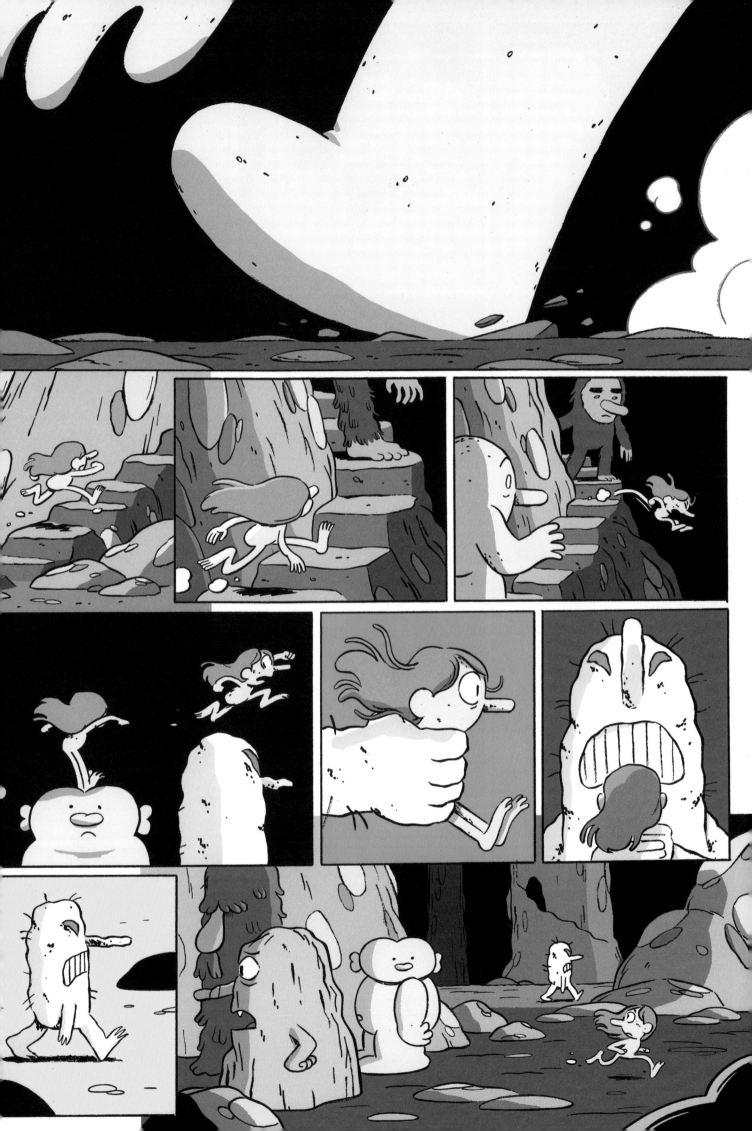

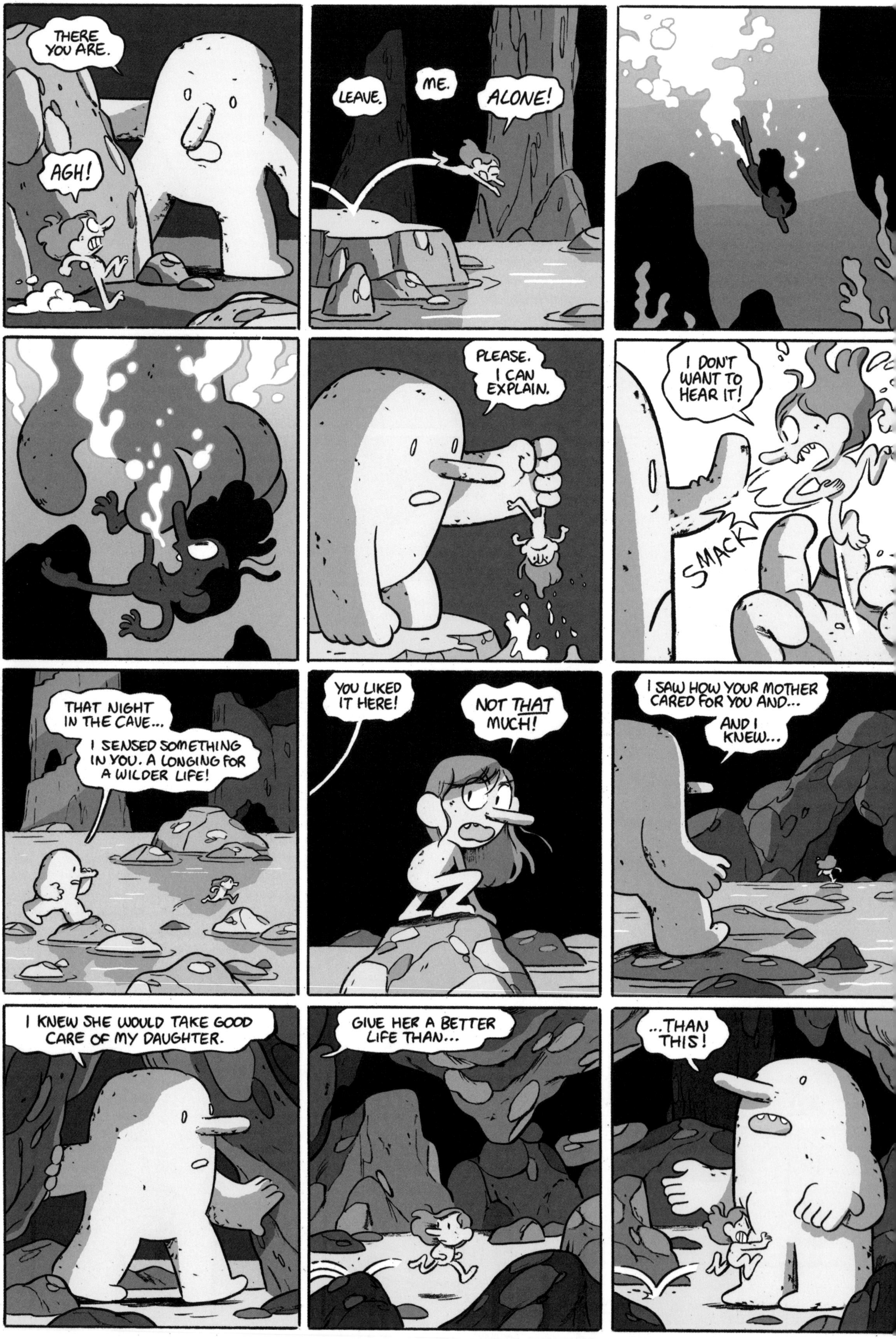
THERE YOU ARE.
AGH!
LEAVE.
ME.
ALONE!
PLEASE. I CAN EXPLAIN.
I DON'T WANT TO HEAR IT!
SMACK
THAT NIGHT IN THE CAVE...
I SENSED SOMETHING IN YOU. A LONGING FOR A WILDER LIFE!
YOU LIKED IT HERE!
NOT THAT MUCH!
I SAW HOW YOUR MOTHER CARED FOR YOU AND...
AND I KNEW...
I KNEW SHE WOULD TAKE GOOD CARE OF MY DAUGHTER.
GIVE HER A BETTER LIFE THAN...
...THAN THIS!

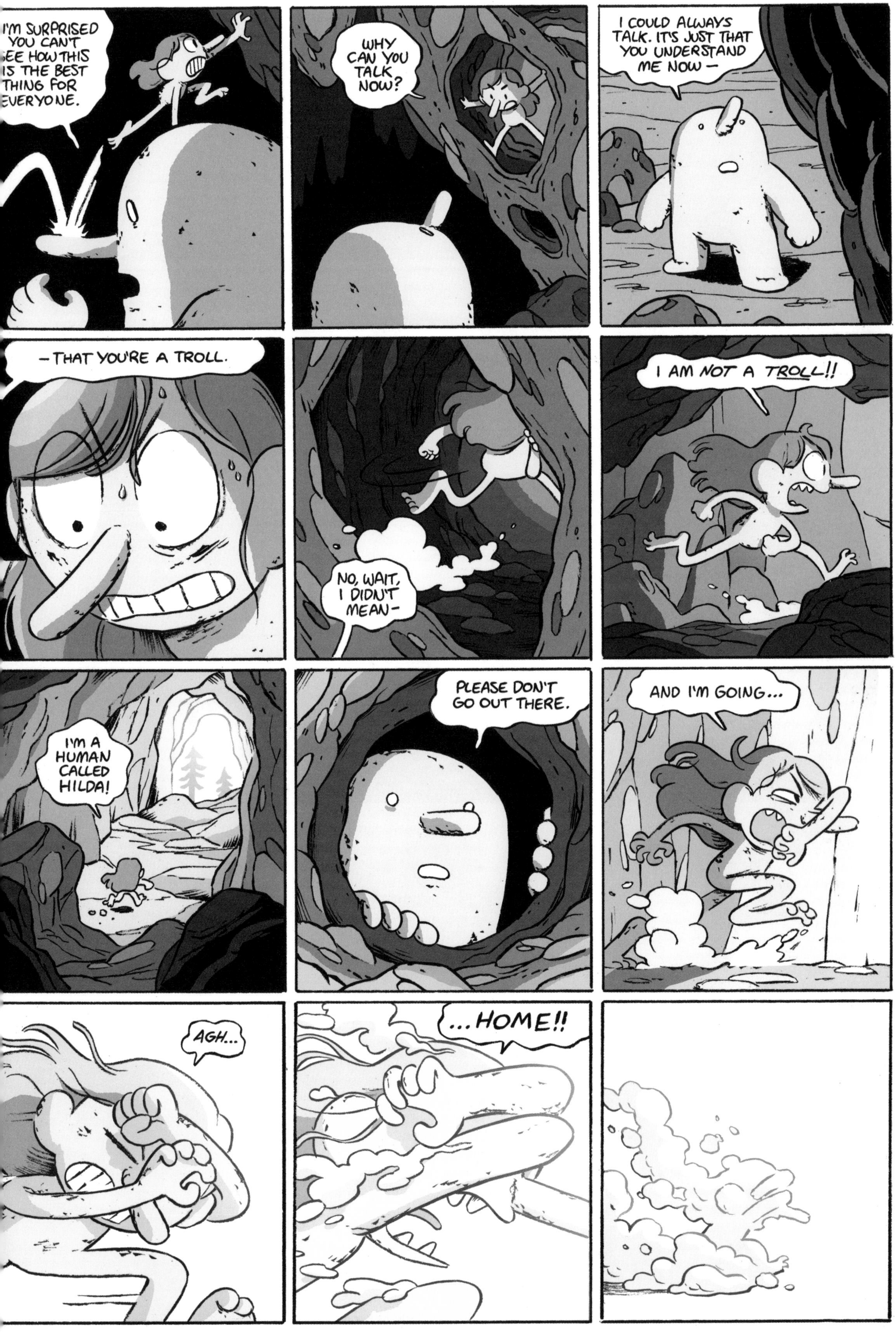
I'M SURPRISED YOU CAN'T SEE HOW THIS IS THE BEST THING FOR EVERYONE.
WHY CAN YOU TALK NOW?
I COULD ALWAYS TALK. IT'S JUST THAT YOU UNDERSTAND ME NOW —
— THAT YOU'RE A TROLL.
NO, WAIT, I DIDN'T MEAN—
I AM NOT A TROLL!!
I'M A HUMAN CALLED HILDA!
PLEASE DON'T GO OUT THERE.
AND I'M GOING...
AGH...
...HOME!!

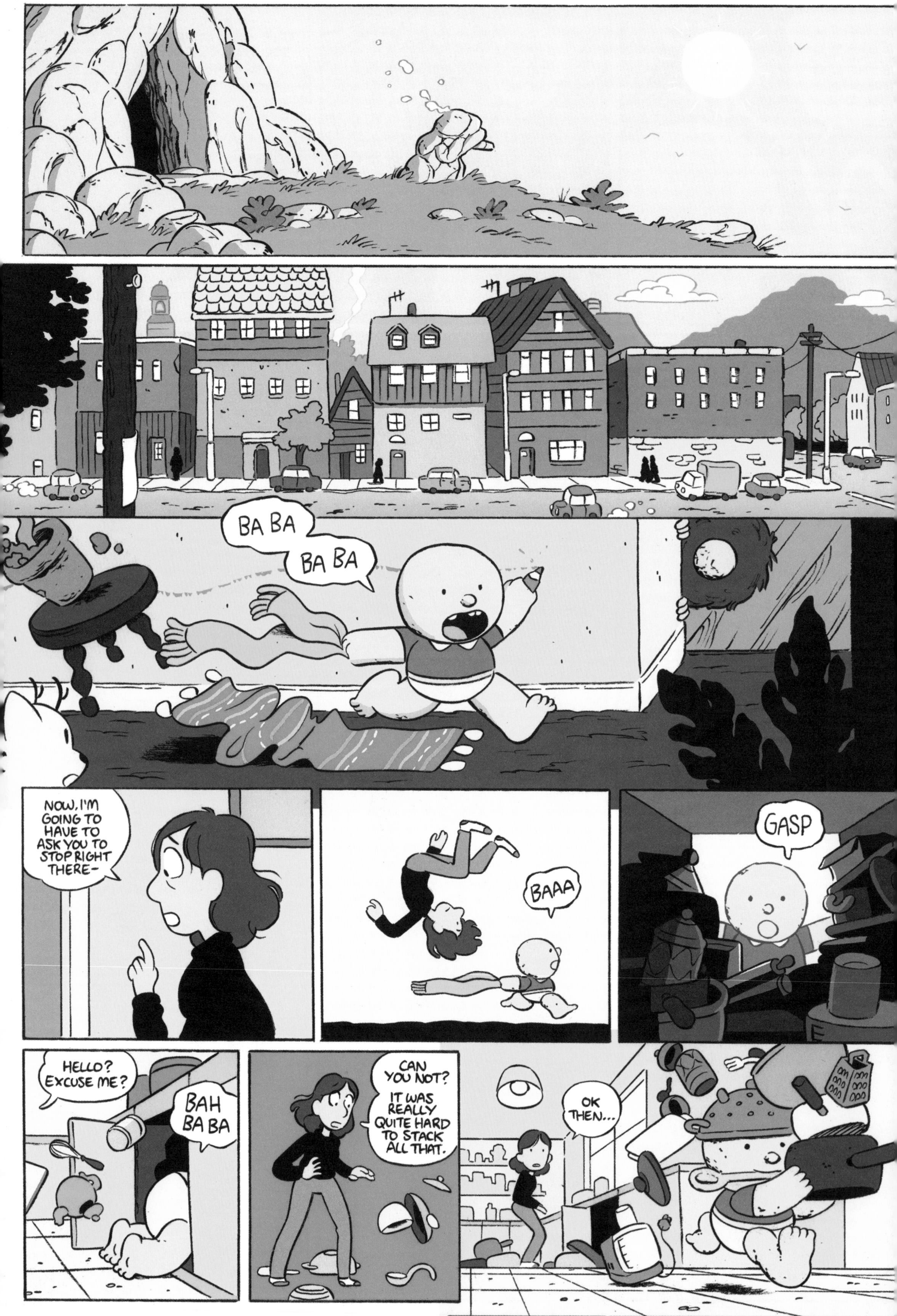
BA BA
BA BA
NOW, I'M GOING TO HAVE TO ASK YOU TO STOP RIGHT THERE-
BAAA
GASP
HELLO? EXCUSE ME?
BAH BA BA
CAN YOU NOT?
IT WAS REALLY QUITE HARD TO STACK ALL THAT.
OK THEN...

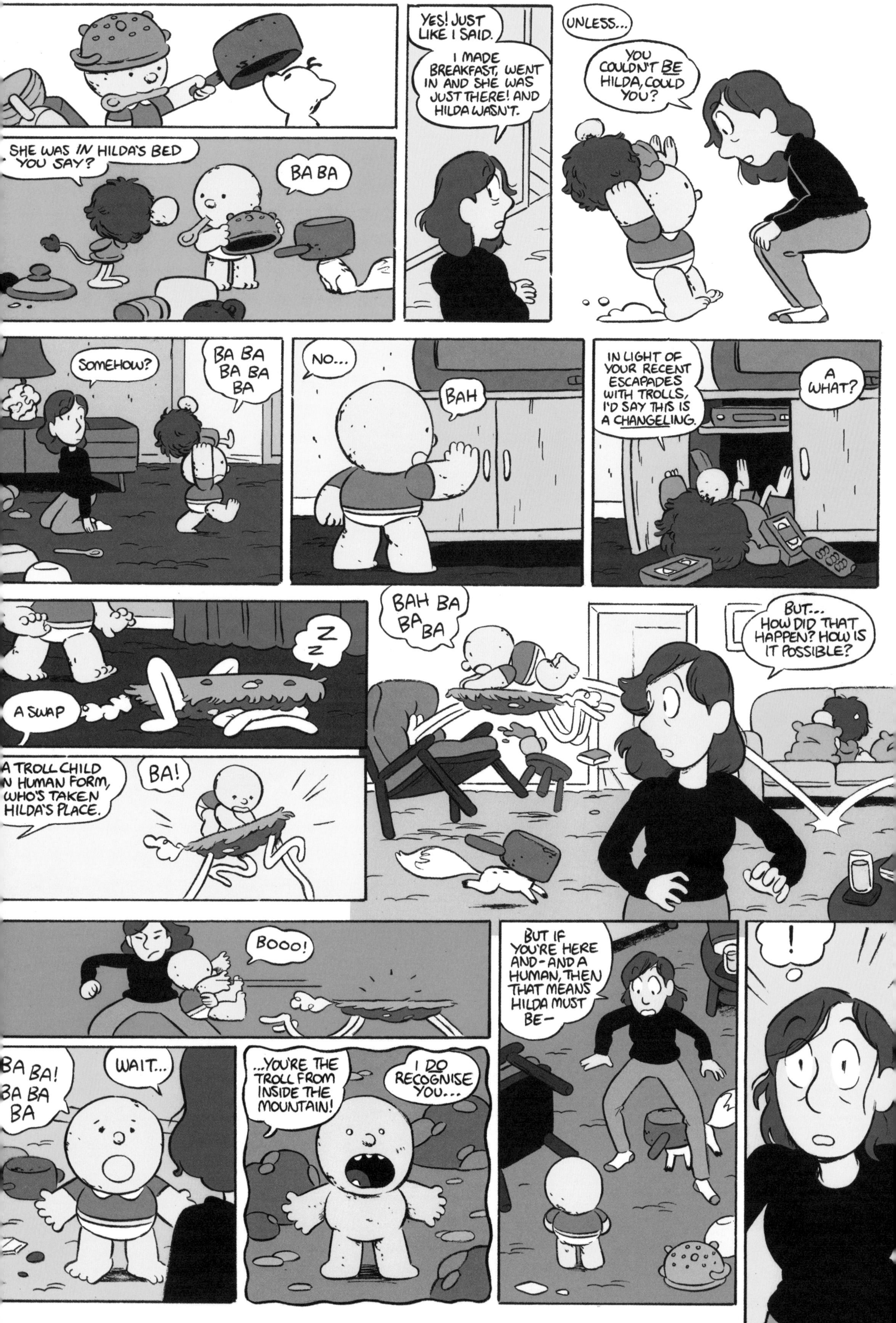
SHE WAS IN HILDA'S BED YOU SAY?
BA BA
YES! JUST LIKE I SAID.
I MADE BREAKFAST, WENT IN AND SHE WAS JUST THERE! AND HILDA WASN'T.
UNLESS...
YOU COULDN'T BE HILDA, COULD YOU?
SOMEHOW?
BA BA BA BA BA
NO...
BAH
IN LIGHT OF YOUR RECENT ESCAPADES WITH TROLLS, I'D SAY THIS IS A CHANGELING.
A WHAT?
A SWAP
A TROLL CHILD IN HUMAN FORM, WHO'S TAKEN HILDA'S PLACE.
BA!
BAH BA BA BA
BUT... HOW DID THAT HAPPEN? HOW IS IT POSSIBLE?
BOOO!
BA BA! BA BA BA
WAIT...
...YOU'RE THE TROLL FROM INSIDE THE MOUNTAIN!
I DO RECOGNISE YOU...
BUT IF YOU'RE HERE AND-AND A HUMAN, THEN THAT MEANS HILDA MUST BE-
!

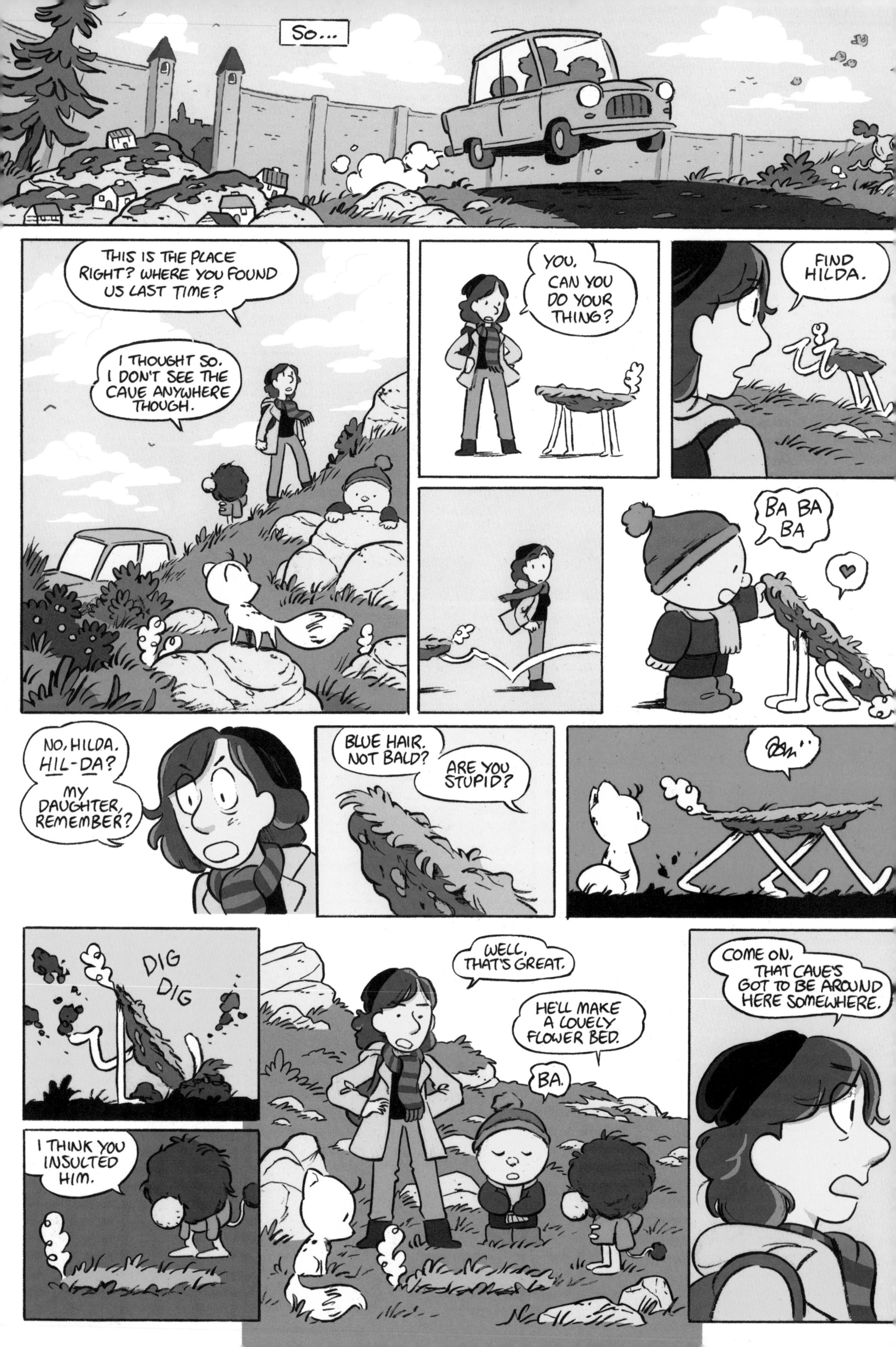
So...
THIS IS THE PLACE RIGHT? WHERE YOU FOUND US LAST TIME?
I THOUGHT SO. I DON'T SEE THE CAVE ANYWHERE THOUGH.
YOU. CAN YOU DO YOUR THING?
FIND HILDA.
BA BA BA
NO, HILDA. HIL-DA?
MY DAUGHTER, REMEMBER?
BLUE HAIR. NOT BALD?
ARE YOU STUPID?
DIG DIG
I THINK YOU INSULTED HIM.
WELL, THAT'S GREAT.
HE'LL MAKE A LOVELY FLOWER BED.
BA.
COME ON. THAT CAVE'S GOT TO BE AROUND HERE SOMEWHERE.

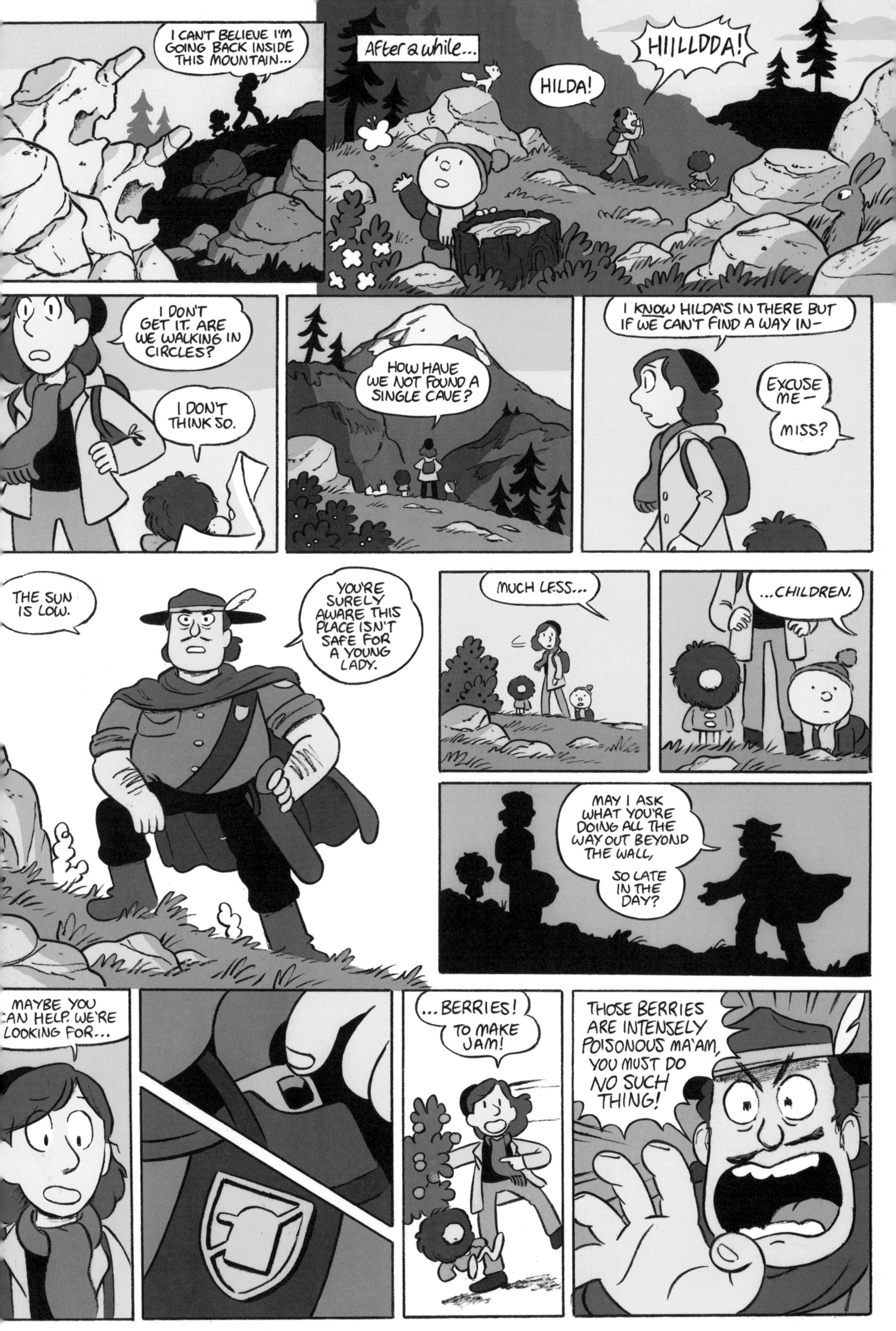

I CAN'T BELIEVE I'M GOING BACK INSIDE THIS MOUNTAIN...
After a while...
HILDA!
HIILLDDA!
I DON'T GET IT. ARE WE WALKING IN CIRCLES?
I DON'T THINK SO.
HOW HAVE WE NOT FOUND A SINGLE CAVE?
I KNOW HILDA'S IN THERE BUT IF WE CAN'T FIND A WAY IN–
EXCUSE ME–
MISS?
THE SUN IS LOW.
YOU'RE SURELY AWARE THIS PLACE ISN'T SAFE FOR A YOUNG LADY.
MUCH LESS...
...CHILDREN.
MAY I ASK WHAT YOU'RE DOING ALL THE WAY OUT BEYOND THE WALL,
SO LATE IN THE DAY?
MAYBE YOU CAN HELP. WE'RE LOOKING FOR...
...BERRIES!
TO MAKE JAM!
THOSE BERRIES ARE INTENSELY POISONOUS MA'AM, YOU MUST DO NO SUCH THING!

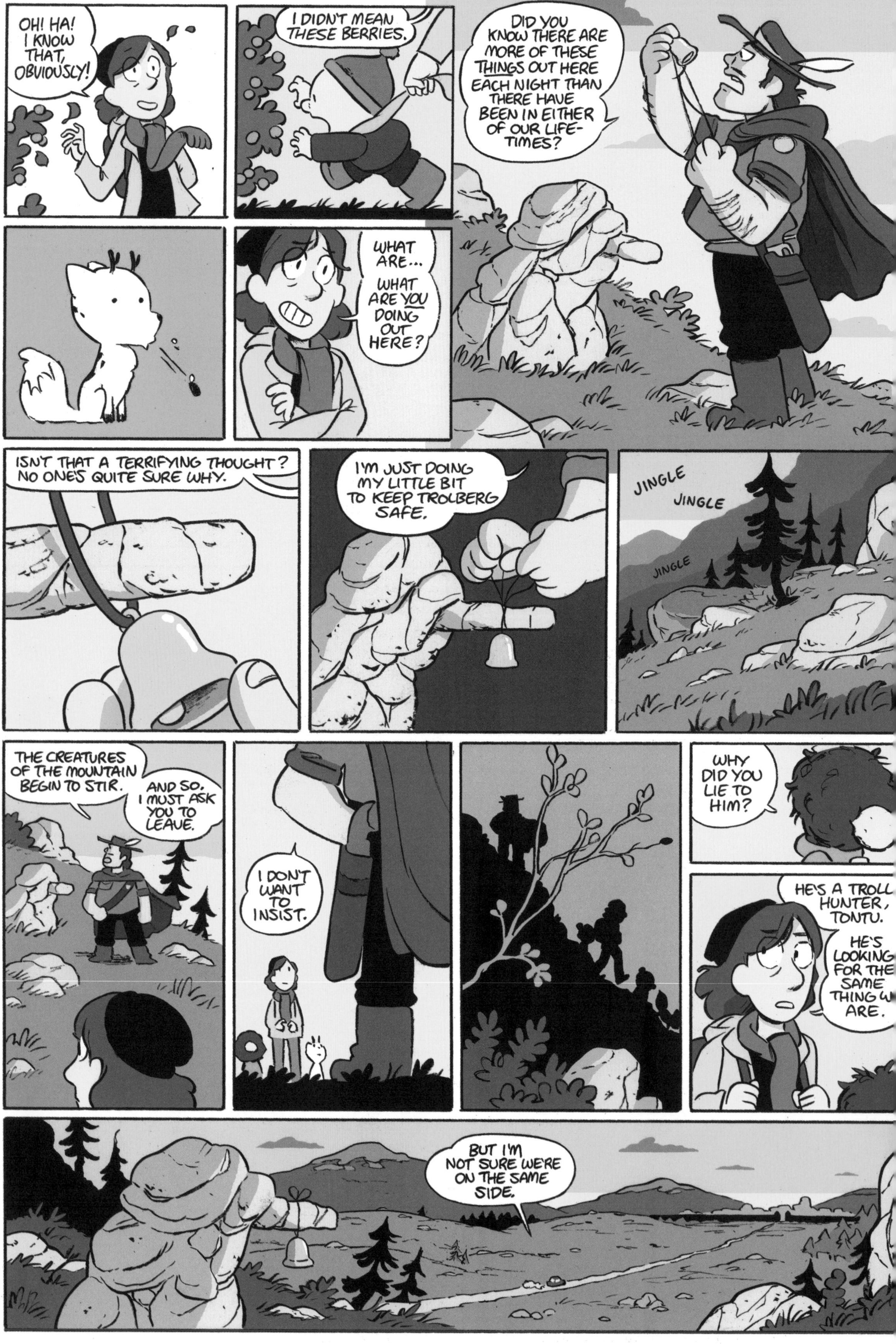
OH! HA! I KNOW THAT, OBVIOUSLY!
I DIDN'T MEAN THESE BERRIES.
DID YOU KNOW THERE ARE MORE OF THESE THINGS OUT HERE EACH NIGHT THAN THERE HAVE BEEN IN EITHER OF OUR LIFE-TIMES?
WHAT ARE...
WHAT ARE YOU DOING OUT HERE?
ISN'T THAT A TERRIFYING THOUGHT? NO ONE'S QUITE SURE WHY.
I'M JUST DOING MY LITTLE BIT TO KEEP TROLBERG SAFE.
JINGLE
JINGLE
JINGLE
THE CREATURES OF THE MOUNTAIN BEGIN TO STIR.
AND SO, I MUST ASK YOU TO LEAVE.
I DON'T WANT TO INSIST.
WHY DID YOU LIE TO HIM?
HE'S A TROLL HUNTER, TONTU.
HE'S LOOKING FOR THE SAME THING W
ARE.
BUT I'M NOT SURE WE'RE ON THE SAME SIDE.

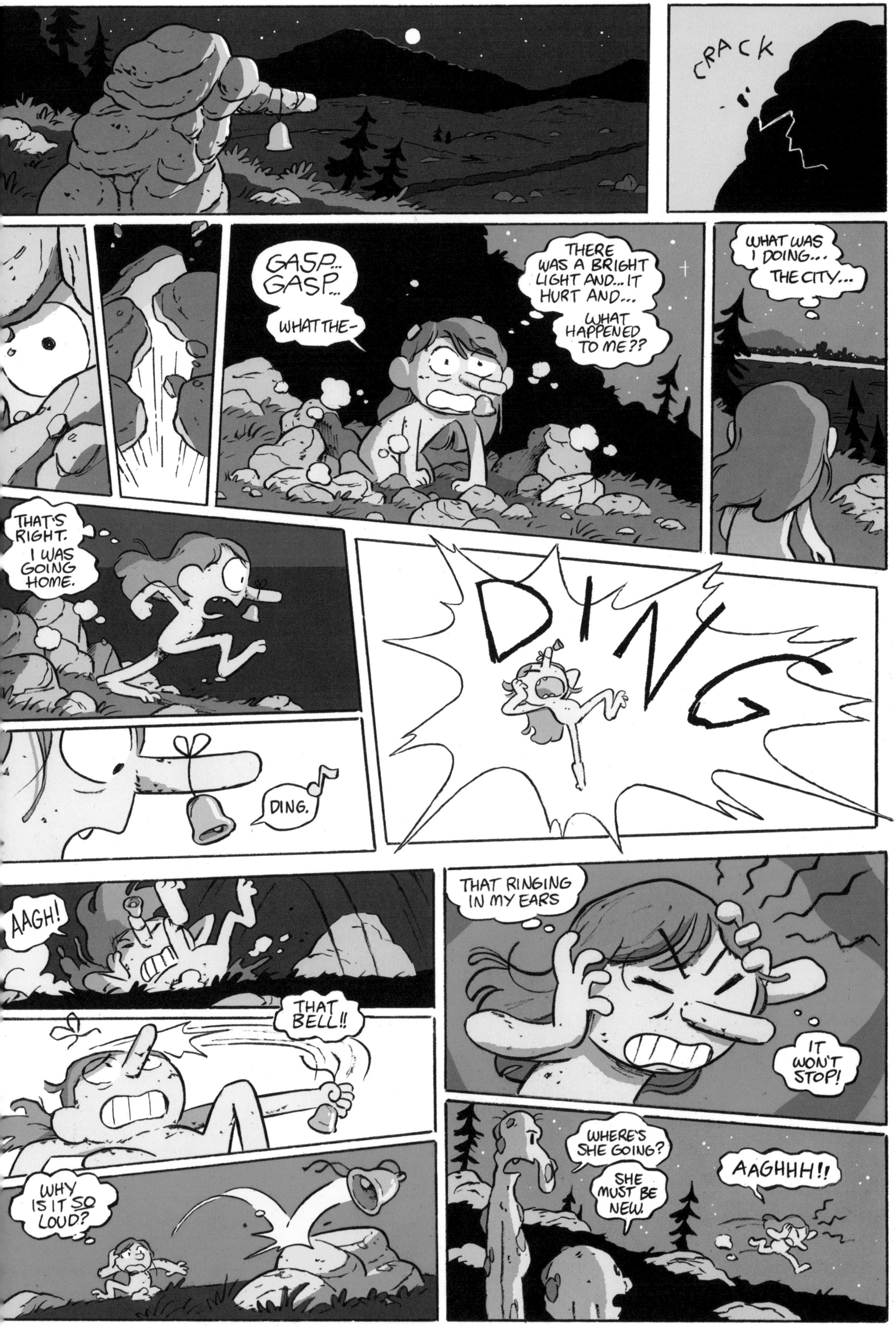
CRACK
GASP... GASP...
WHAT THE-
THERE WAS A BRIGHT LIGHT AND... IT HURT AND...
WHAT HAPPENED TO ME??
WHAT WAS I DOING... THE CITY...
THAT'S RIGHT. I WAS GOING HOME.
DING.
DING
AAGH!
THAT BELL!!
WHY IS IT SO LOUD?
THAT RINGING IN MY EARS
IT WON'T STOP!
WHERE'S SHE GOING?
SHE MUST BE NEW.
AAGHHH!!

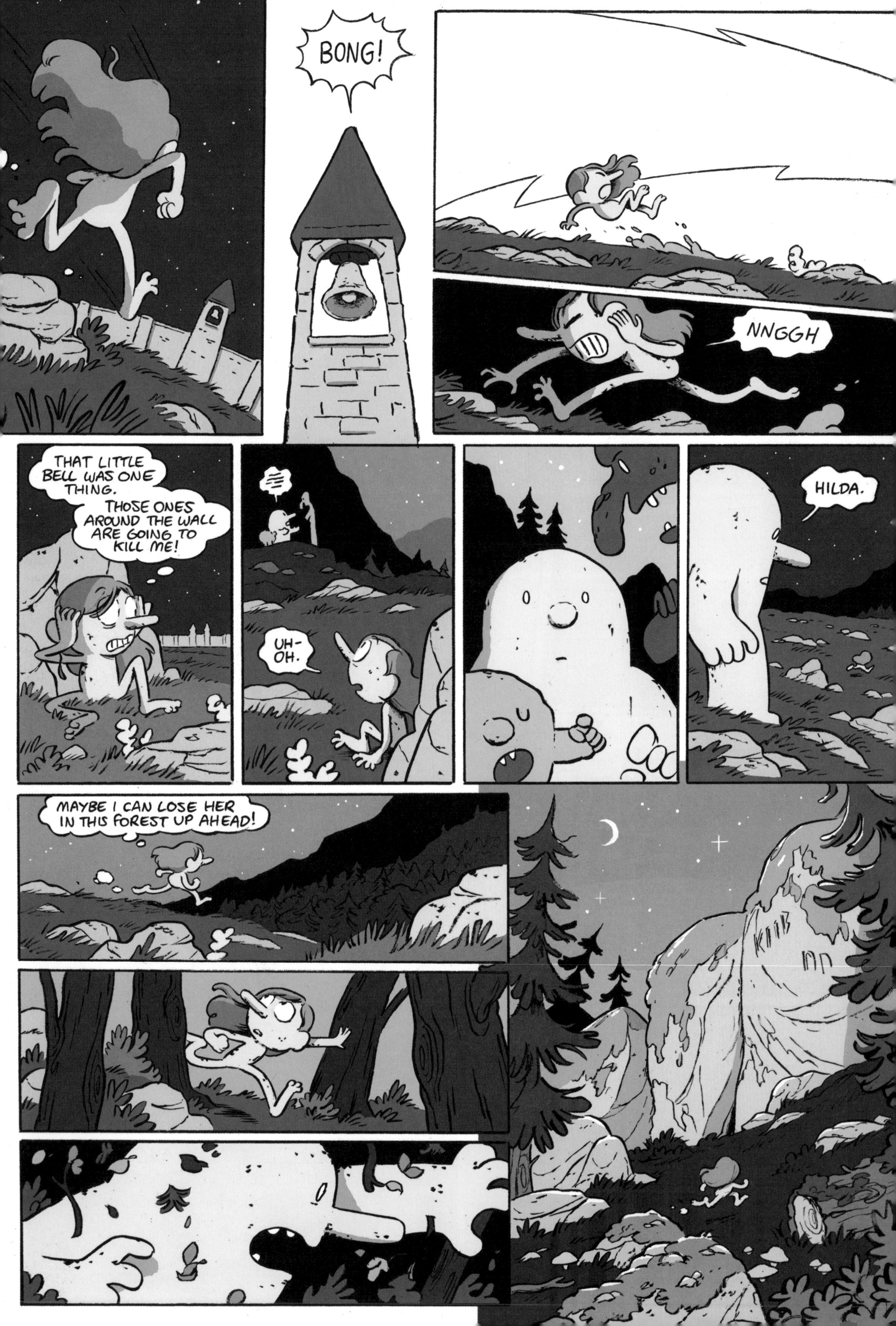
BONG!
NNGGH
THAT LITTLE BELL WAS ONE THING.
THOSE ONES AROUND THE WALL ARE GOING TO KILL ME!
UH-OH.
HILDA.
MAYBE I CAN LOSE HER IN THIS FOREST UP AHEAD!

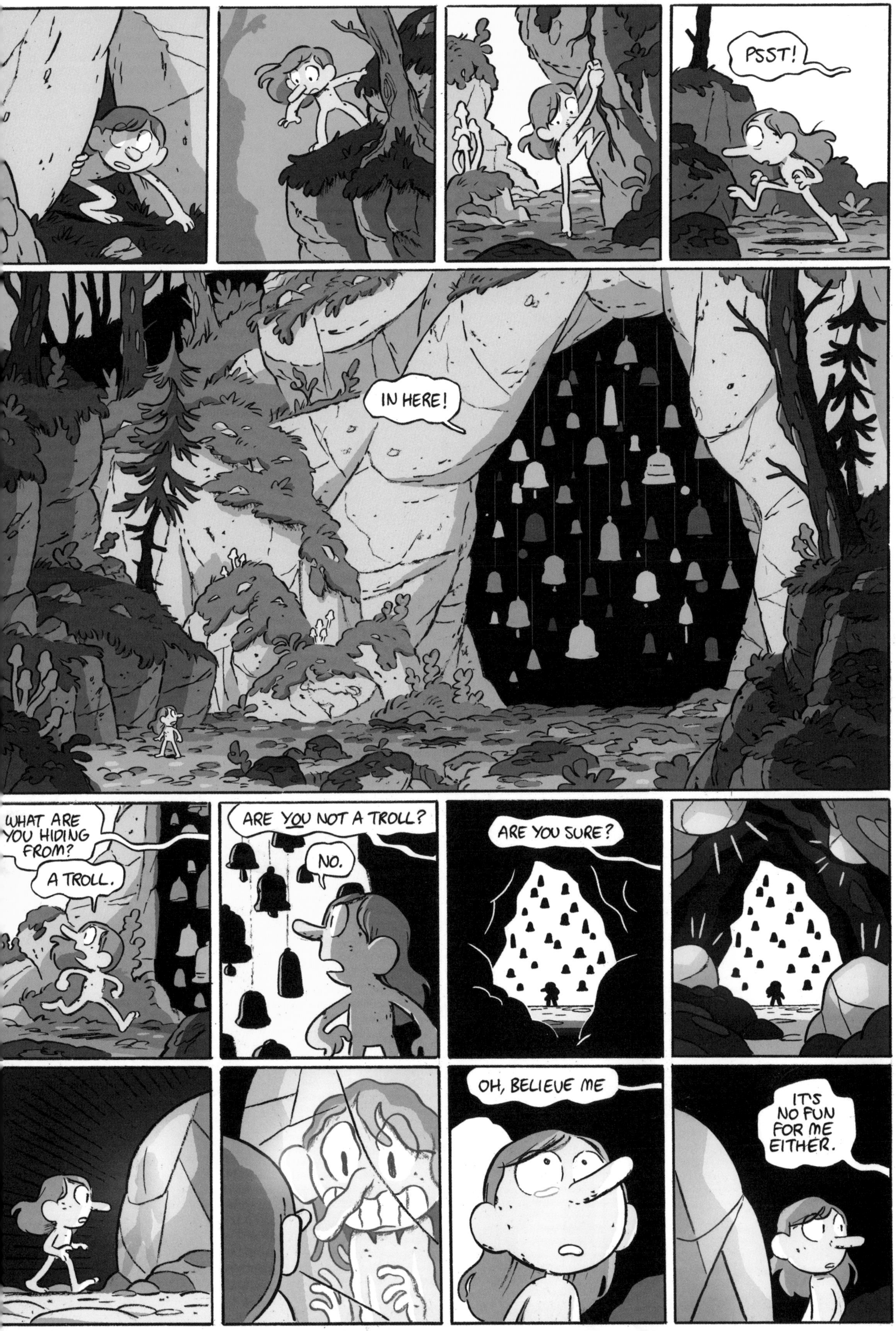
PSST!
IN HERE!
WHAT ARE YOU HIDING FROM?
A TROLL.
ARE YOU NOT A TROLL?
NO.
ARE YOU SURE?
OH, BELIEVE ME
IT'S NO FUN FOR ME EITHER.

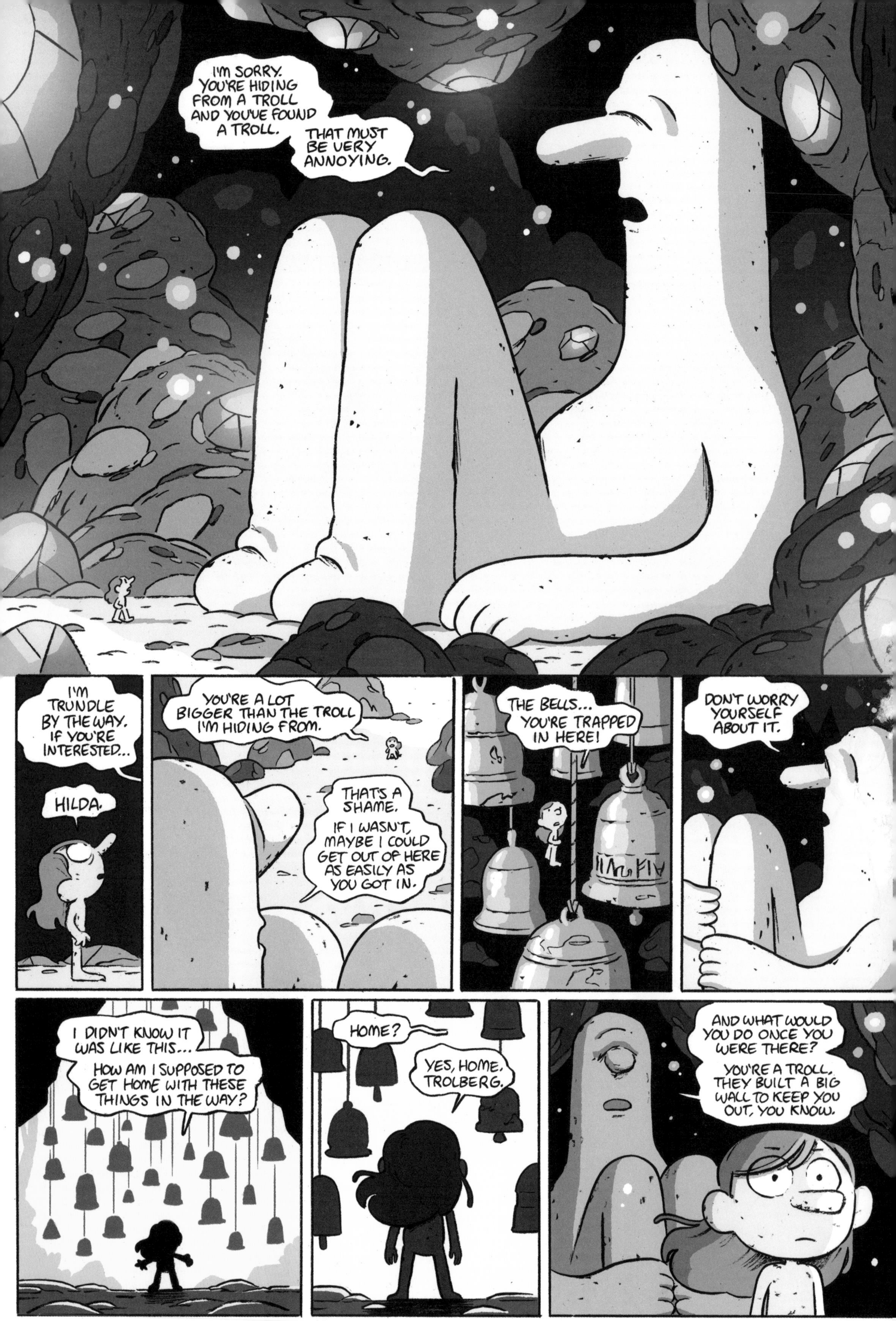

I'M SORRY. YOU'RE HIDING FROM A TROLL AND YOU'VE FOUND A TROLL.
THAT MUST BE VERY ANNOYING.
I'M TRUNDLE BY THE WAY. IF YOU'RE INTERESTED...
HILDA.
YOU'RE A LOT BIGGER THAN THE TROLL I'M HIDING FROM.
THAT'S A SHAME.
IF I WASN'T, MAYBE I COULD GET OUT OF HERE AS EASILY AS YOU GOT IN.
THE BELLS... YOU'RE TRAPPED IN HERE!
DON'T WORRY YOURSELF ABOUT IT.
I DIDN'T KNOW IT WAS LIKE THIS...
HOW AM I SUPPOSED TO GET HOME WITH THESE THINGS IN THE WAY?
HOME?
YES, HOME. TROLBERG.
AND WHAT WOULD YOU DO ONCE YOU WERE THERE?
YOU'RE A TROLL. THEY BUILT A BIG WALL TO KEEP YOU OUT, YOU KNOW.

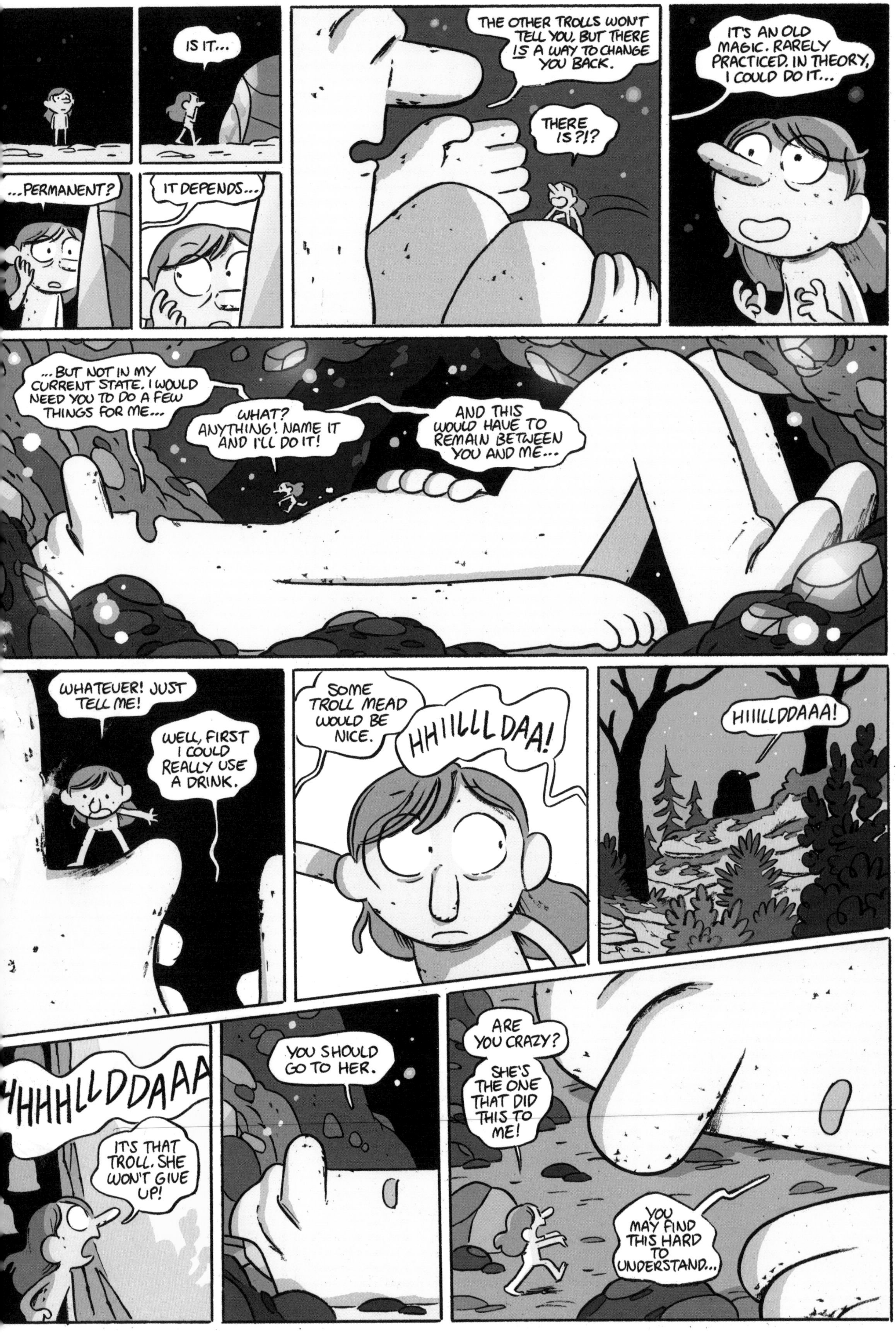
IS IT...
...PERMANENT?
IT DEPENDS...
THE OTHER TROLLS WON'T TELL YOU, BUT THERE IS A WAY TO CHANGE YOU BACK.
THERE IS?!?
IT'S AN OLD MAGIC. RARELY PRACTICED. IN THEORY, I COULD DO IT...
...BUT NOT IN MY CURRENT STATE. I WOULD NEED YOU TO DO A FEW THINGS FOR ME...
WHAT? ANYTHING! NAME IT AND I'LL DO IT!
AND THIS WOULD HAVE TO REMAIN BETWEEN YOU AND ME...
WHATEVER! JUST TELL ME!
WELL, FIRST I COULD REALLY USE A DRINK.
SOME TROLL MEAD WOULD BE NICE.
HHIILLLDAA!
HIIILLDDAAA!
HHHHLLDDAAA
IT'S THAT TROLL. SHE WON'T GIVE UP!
YOU SHOULD GO TO HER.
ARE YOU CRAZY?
SHE'S THE ONE THAT DID THIS TO ME!
YOU MAY FIND THIS HARD TO UNDERSTAND...

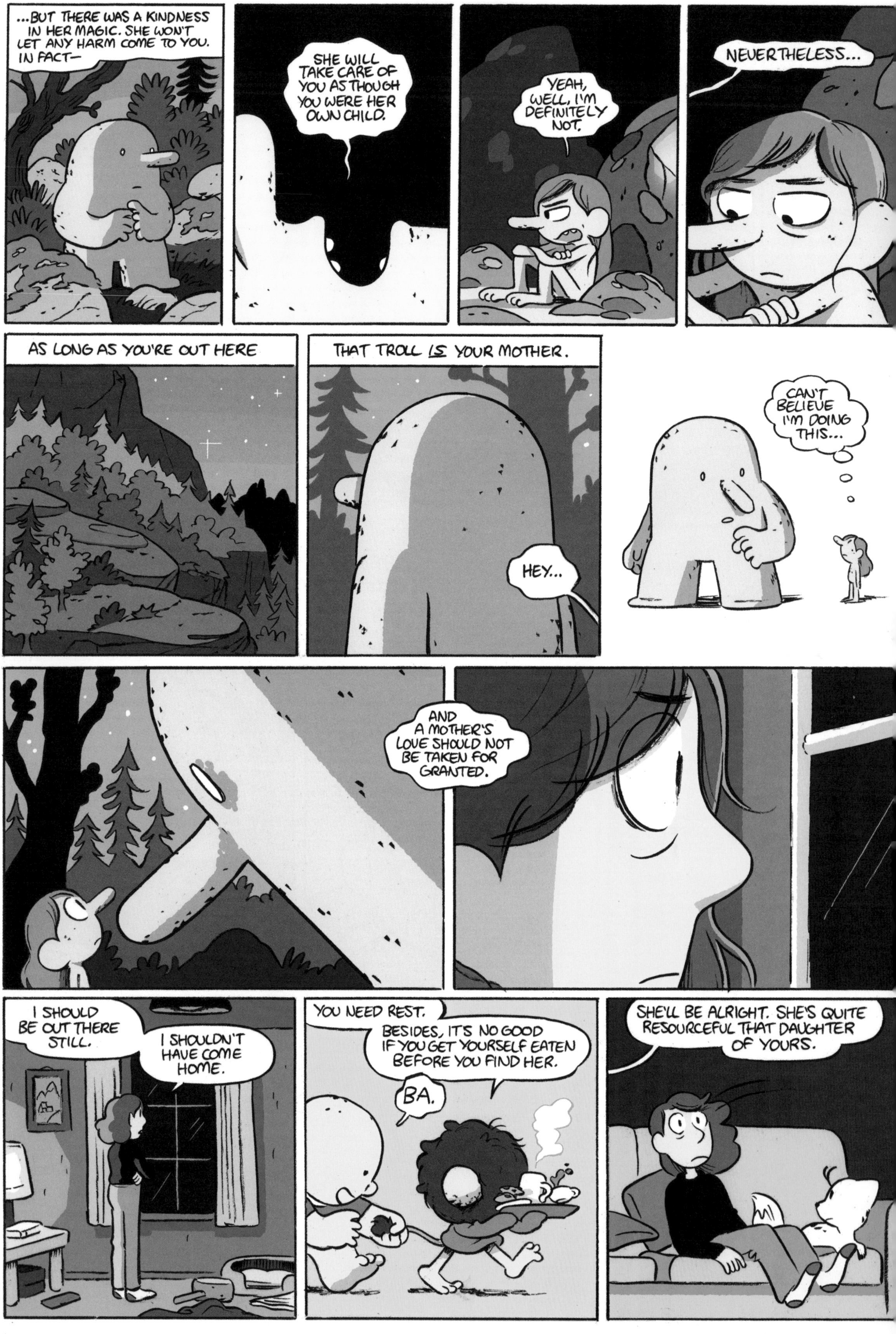
...BUT THERE WAS A KINDNESS IN HER MAGIC. SHE WON'T LET ANY HARM COME TO YOU. IN FACT—
SHE WILL TAKE CARE OF YOU AS THOUGH YOU WERE HER OWN CHILD.
YEAH, WELL, I'M DEFINITELY NOT.
NEVERTHELESS...
AS LONG AS YOU'RE OUT HERE
THAT TROLL IS YOUR MOTHER.
HEY...
CAN'T BELIEVE I'M DOING THIS...
AND A MOTHER'S LOVE SHOULD NOT BE TAKEN FOR GRANTED.
I SHOULD BE OUT THERE STILL.
I SHOULDN'T HAVE COME HOME.
YOU NEED REST.
BESIDES, IT'S NO GOOD IF YOU GET YOURSELF EATEN BEFORE YOU FIND HER.
BA.
SHE'LL BE ALRIGHT. SHE'S QUITE RESOURCEFUL THAT DAUGHTER OF YOURS.

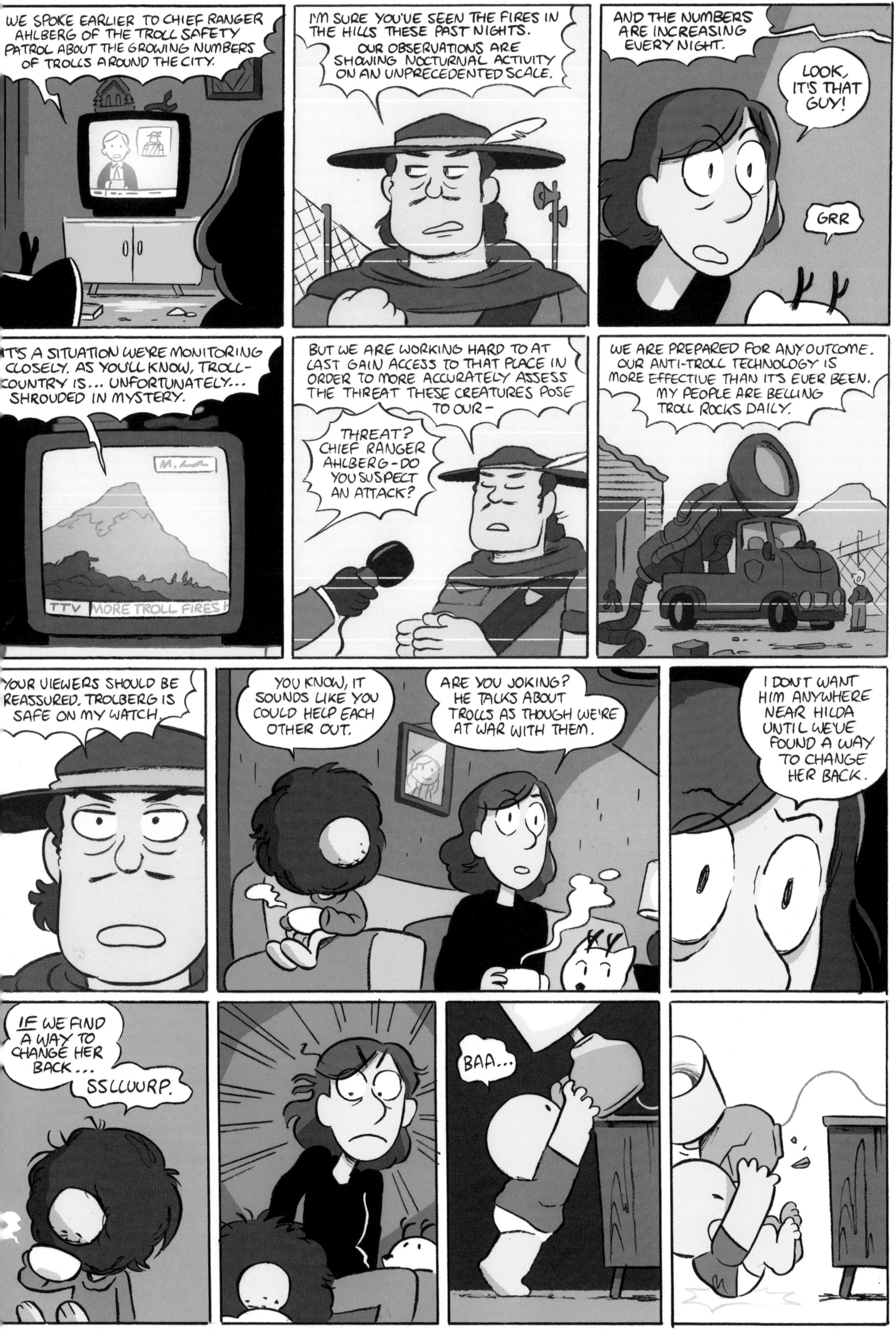
WE SPOKE EARLIER TO CHIEF RANGER AHLBERG OF THE TROLL SAFETY PATROL ABOUT THE GROWING NUMBERS OF TROLLS AROUND THE CITY.
I'M SURE YOU'VE SEEN THE FIRES IN THE HILLS THESE PAST NIGHTS.
OUR OBSERVATIONS ARE SHOWING NOCTURNAL ACTIVITY ON AN UNPRECEDENTED SCALE.
AND THE NUMBERS ARE INCREASING EVERY NIGHT.
LOOK, IT'S THAT GUY!
GRR
IT'S A SITUATION WE'RE MONITORING CLOSELY. AS YOU'LL KNOW, TROLL-COUNTRY IS... UNFORTUNATELY... SHROUDED IN MYSTERY.
TTV MORE TROLL FIRES
BUT WE ARE WORKING HARD TO AT LAST GAIN ACCESS TO THAT PLACE IN ORDER TO MORE ACCURATELY ASSESS THE THREAT THESE CREATURES POSE TO OUR–
THREAT? CHIEF RANGER AHLBERG–DO YOU SUSPECT AN ATTACK?
WE ARE PREPARED FOR ANY OUTCOME. OUR ANTI-TROLL TECHNOLOGY IS MORE EFFECTIVE THAN IT'S EVER BEEN. MY PEOPLE ARE BELLING TROLL ROCKS DAILY.
YOUR VIEWERS SHOULD BE REASSURED. TROLBERG IS SAFE ON MY WATCH.
YOU KNOW, IT SOUNDS LIKE YOU COULD HELP EACH OTHER OUT.
ARE YOU JOKING? HE TALKS ABOUT TROLLS AS THOUGH WE'RE AT WAR WITH THEM.
I DON'T WANT HIM ANYWHERE NEAR HILDA UNTIL WE'VE FOUND A WAY TO CHANGE HER BACK.
IF WE FIND A WAY TO CHANGE HER BACK...
SSLLUURP.
BAA...

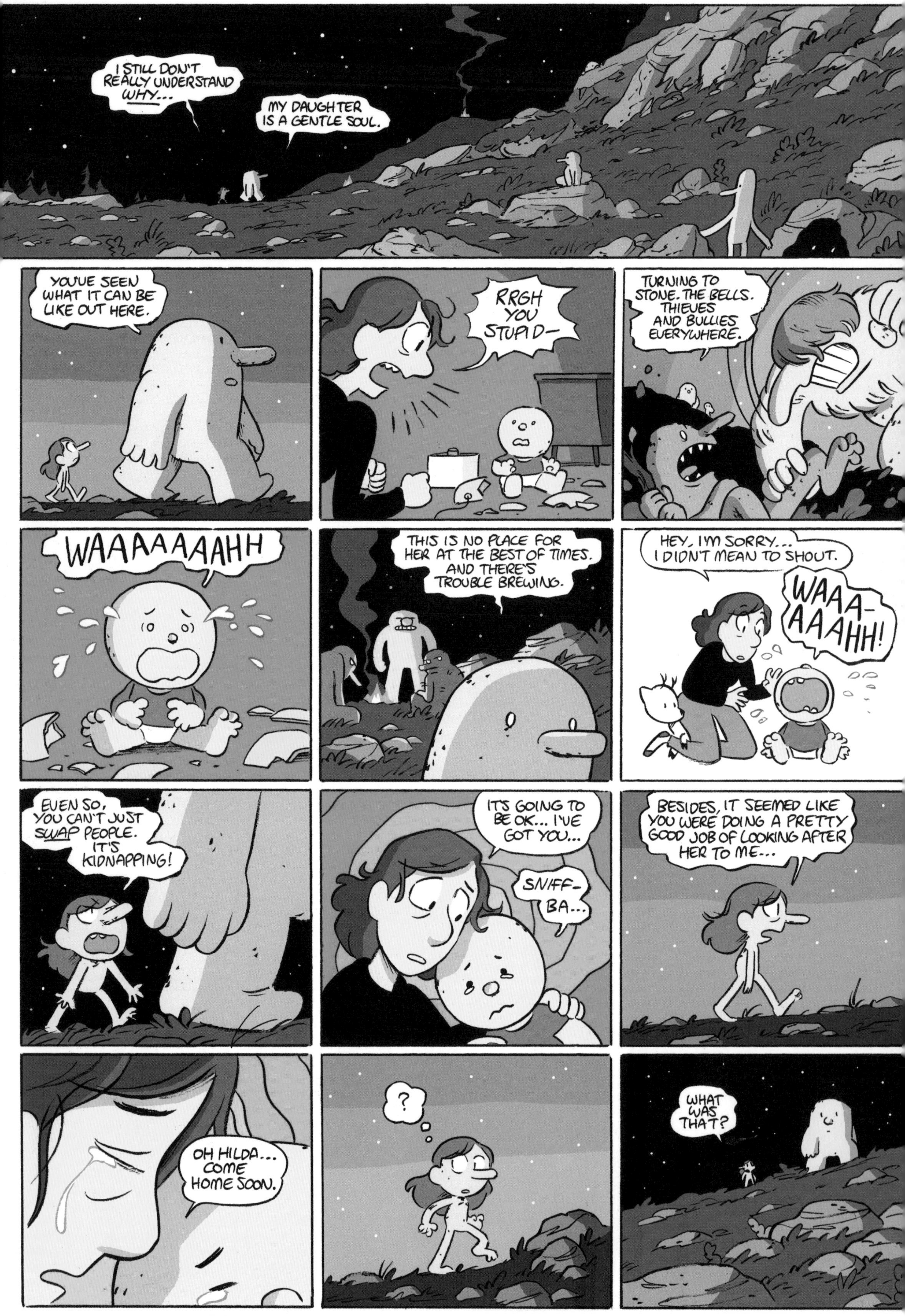

I STILL DON'T REALLY UNDERSTAND WHY...
MY DAUGHTER IS A GENTLE SOUL.
YOU'VE SEEN WHAT IT CAN BE LIKE OUT HERE.
RRGH YOU STUPID—
TURNING TO STONE. THE BELLS. THIEVES AND BULLIES EVERYWHERE.
WAAAAAAAHH
THIS IS NO PLACE FOR HER AT THE BEST OF TIMES. AND THERE'S TROUBLE BREWING.
HEY, I'M SORRY... I DIDN'T MEAN TO SHOUT.
WAAA-AAAHH!
EVEN SO, YOU CAN'T JUST SWAP PEOPLE. IT'S KIDNAPPING!
IT'S GOING TO BE OK... I'VE GOT YOU...
SNIFF-BA...
BESIDES, IT SEEMED LIKE YOU WERE DOING A PRETTY GOOD JOB OF LOOKING AFTER HER TO ME...
OH HILDA... COME HOME SOON.
?
WHAT WAS THAT?

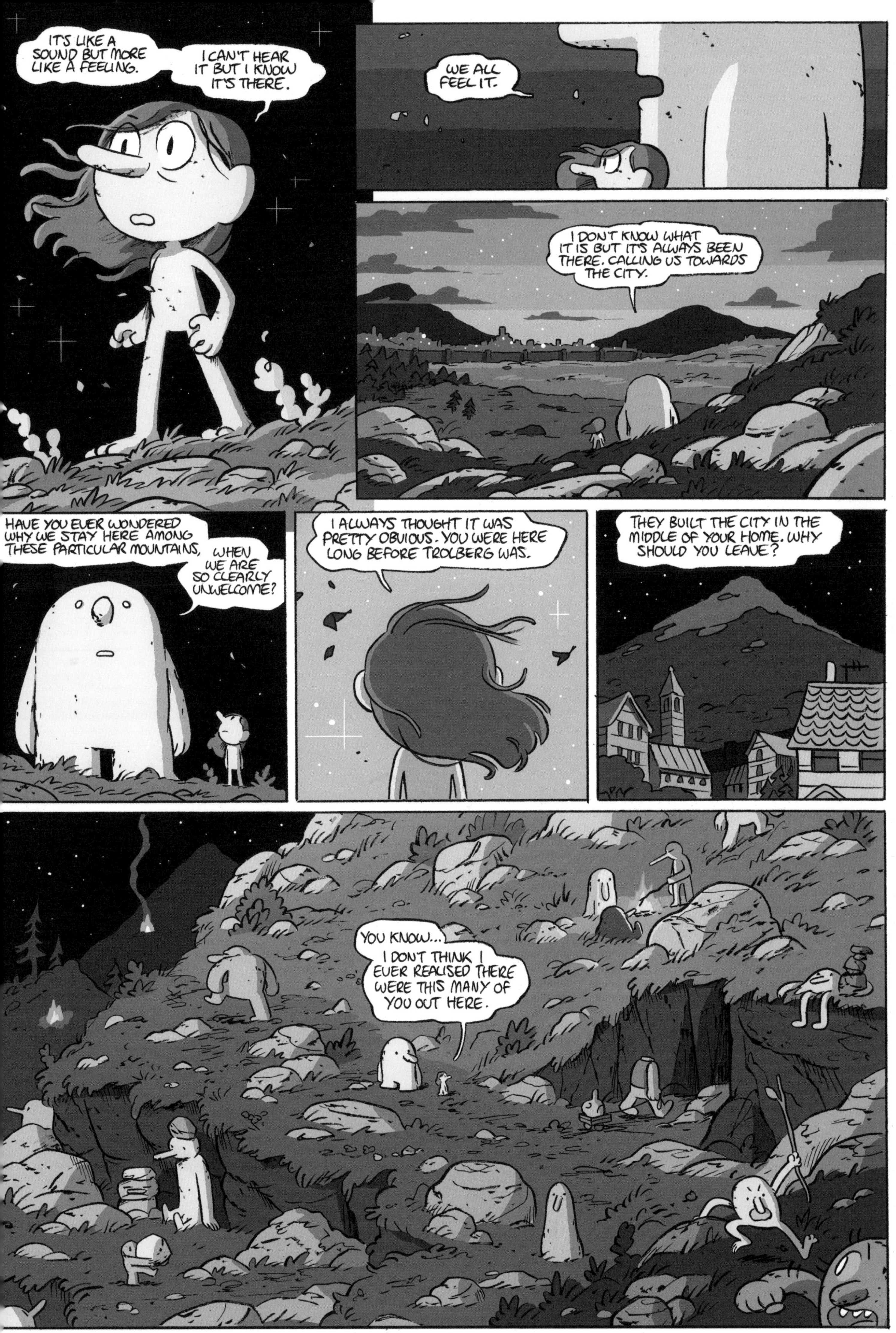
IT'S LIKE A SOUND BUT MORE LIKE A FEELING.
I CAN'T HEAR IT BUT I KNOW IT'S THERE.
WE ALL FEEL IT.
I DON'T KNOW WHAT IT IS BUT IT'S ALWAYS BEEN THERE. CALLING US TOWARDS THE CITY.
HAVE YOU EVER WONDERED WHY WE STAY HERE AMONG THESE PARTICULAR MOUNTAINS,
WHEN WE ARE SO CLEARLY UNWELCOME?
I ALWAYS THOUGHT IT WAS PRETTY OBVIOUS. YOU WERE HERE LONG BEFORE TROLBERG WAS.
THEY BUILT THE CITY IN THE MIDDLE OF YOUR HOME. WHY SHOULD YOU LEAVE?
YOU KNOW...
I DON'T THINK I EVER REALISED THERE WERE THIS MANY OF YOU OUT HERE.

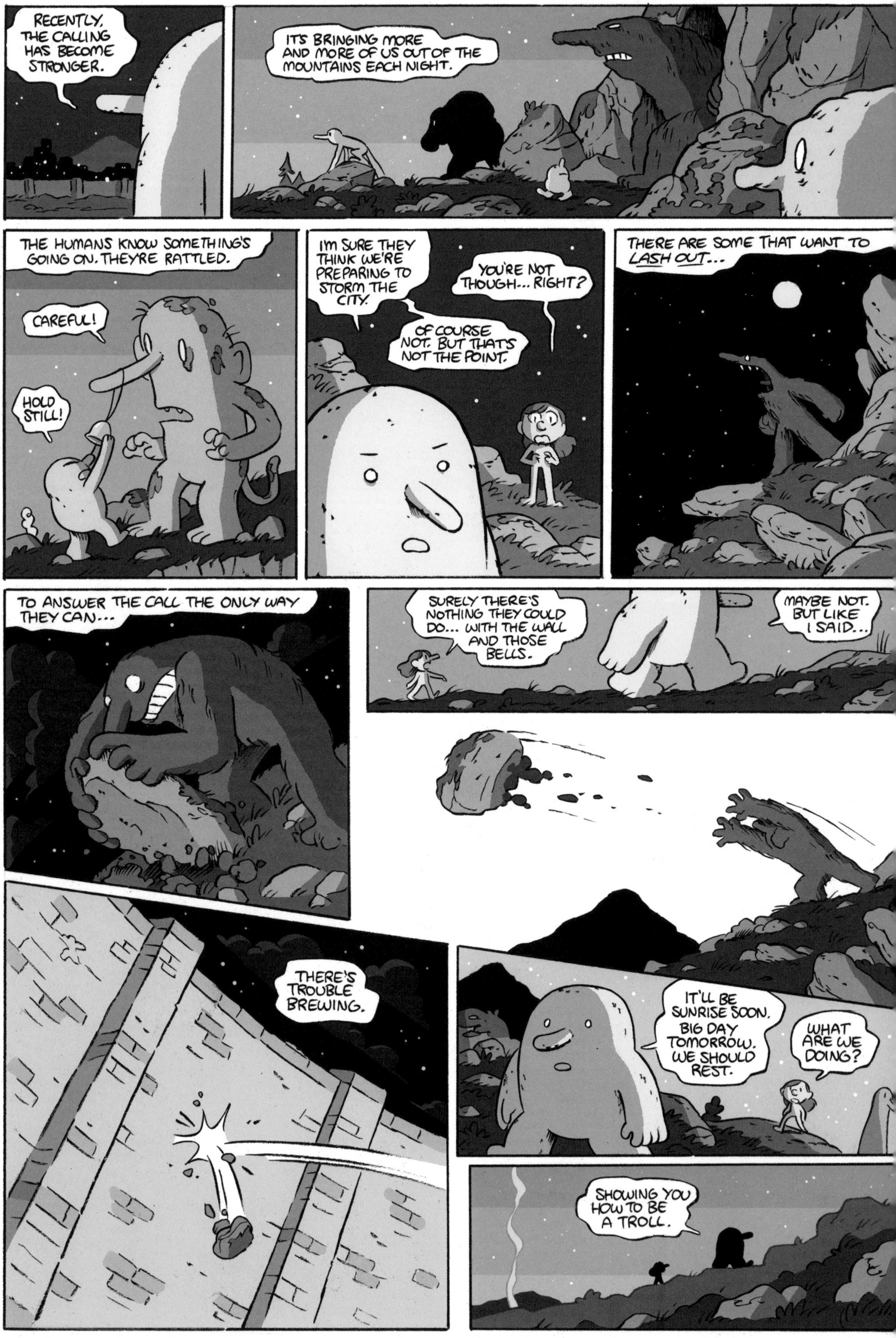
RECENTLY, THE CALLING HAS BECOME STRONGER.
IT'S BRINGING MORE AND MORE OF US OUT OF THE MOUNTAINS EACH NIGHT.
THE HUMANS KNOW SOMETHING'S GOING ON. THEY'RE RATTLED.
CAREFUL!
HOLD STILL!
I'M SURE THEY THINK WE'RE PREPARING TO STORM THE CITY.
YOU'RE NOT THOUGH... RIGHT?
OF COURSE NOT. BUT THAT'S NOT THE POINT.
THERE ARE SOME THAT WANT TO LASH OUT...
TO ANSWER THE CALL THE ONLY WAY THEY CAN...
SURELY THERE'S NOTHING THEY COULD DO... WITH THE WALL AND THOSE BELLS.
MAYBE NOT. BUT LIKE I SAID...
THERE'S TROUBLE BREWING.
IT'LL BE SUNRISE SOON. BIG DAY TOMORROW. WE SHOULD REST.
WHAT ARE WE DOING?
SHOWING YOU HOW TO BE A TROLL.

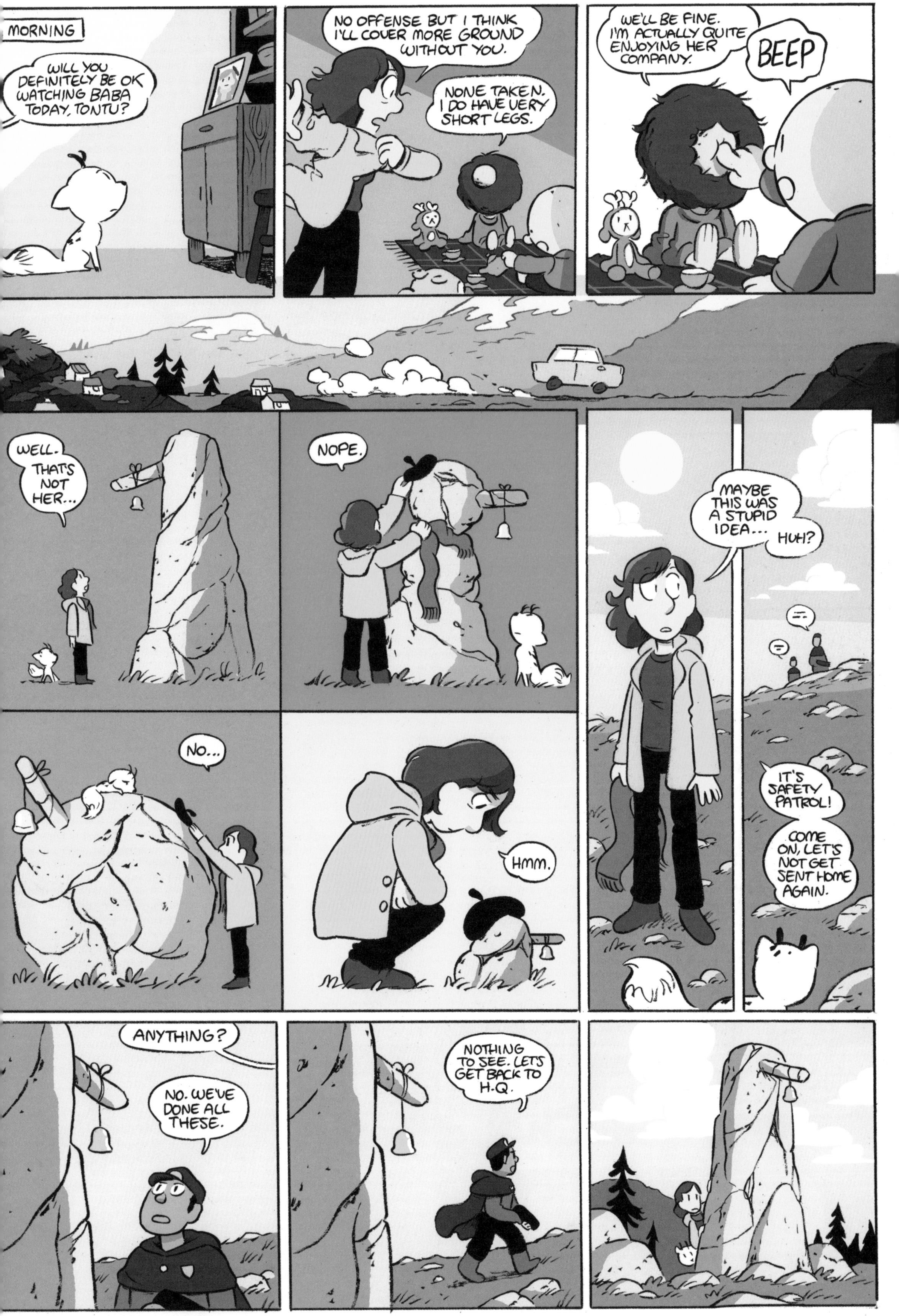
MORNING
WILL YOU DEFINITELY BE OK WATCHING BABA TODAY, TONTU?
NO OFFENSE BUT I THINK I'LL COVER MORE GROUND WITHOUT YOU.
NONE TAKEN. I DO HAVE VERY SHORT LEGS.
WE'LL BE FINE. I'M ACTUALLY QUITE ENJOYING HER COMPANY.
BEEP
WELL. THAT'S NOT HER...
NOPE.
MAYBE THIS WAS A STUPID IDEA...
HUH?
NO...
HMM.
IT'S SAFETY PATROL!
COME ON, LET'S NOT GET SENT HOME AGAIN.
ANYTHING?
NO. WE'VE DONE ALL THESE.
NOTHING TO SEE. LET'S GET BACK TO H.Q.

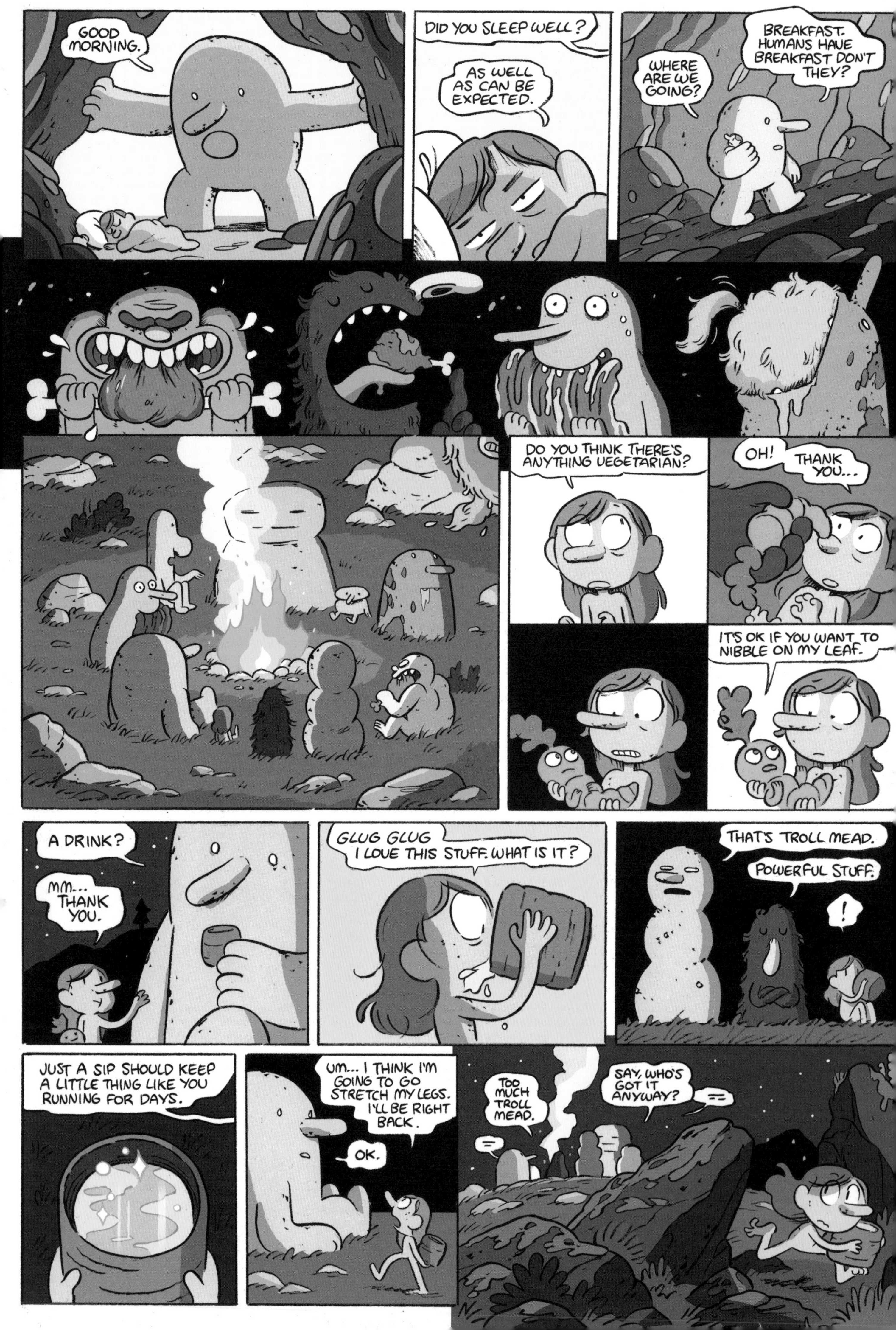
GOOD MORNING.
DID YOU SLEEP WELL?
AS WELL AS CAN BE EXPECTED.
WHERE ARE WE GOING?
BREAKFAST. HUMANS HAVE BREAKFAST DON'T THEY?
DO YOU THINK THERE'S ANYTHING VEGETARIAN?
OH!
THANK YOU...
IT'S OK IF YOU WANT TO NIBBLE ON MY LEAF.
A DRINK?
MM... THANK YOU.
GLUG GLUG
I LOVE THIS STUFF. WHAT IS IT?
THAT'S TROLL MEAD.
POWERFUL STUFF.
!
JUST A SIP SHOULD KEEP A LITTLE THING LIKE YOU RUNNING FOR DAYS.
UM... I THINK I'M GOING TO GO STRETCH MY LEGS. I'LL BE RIGHT BACK.
OK.
TOO MUCH TROLL MEAD.
SAY, WHO'S GOT IT ANYWAY?

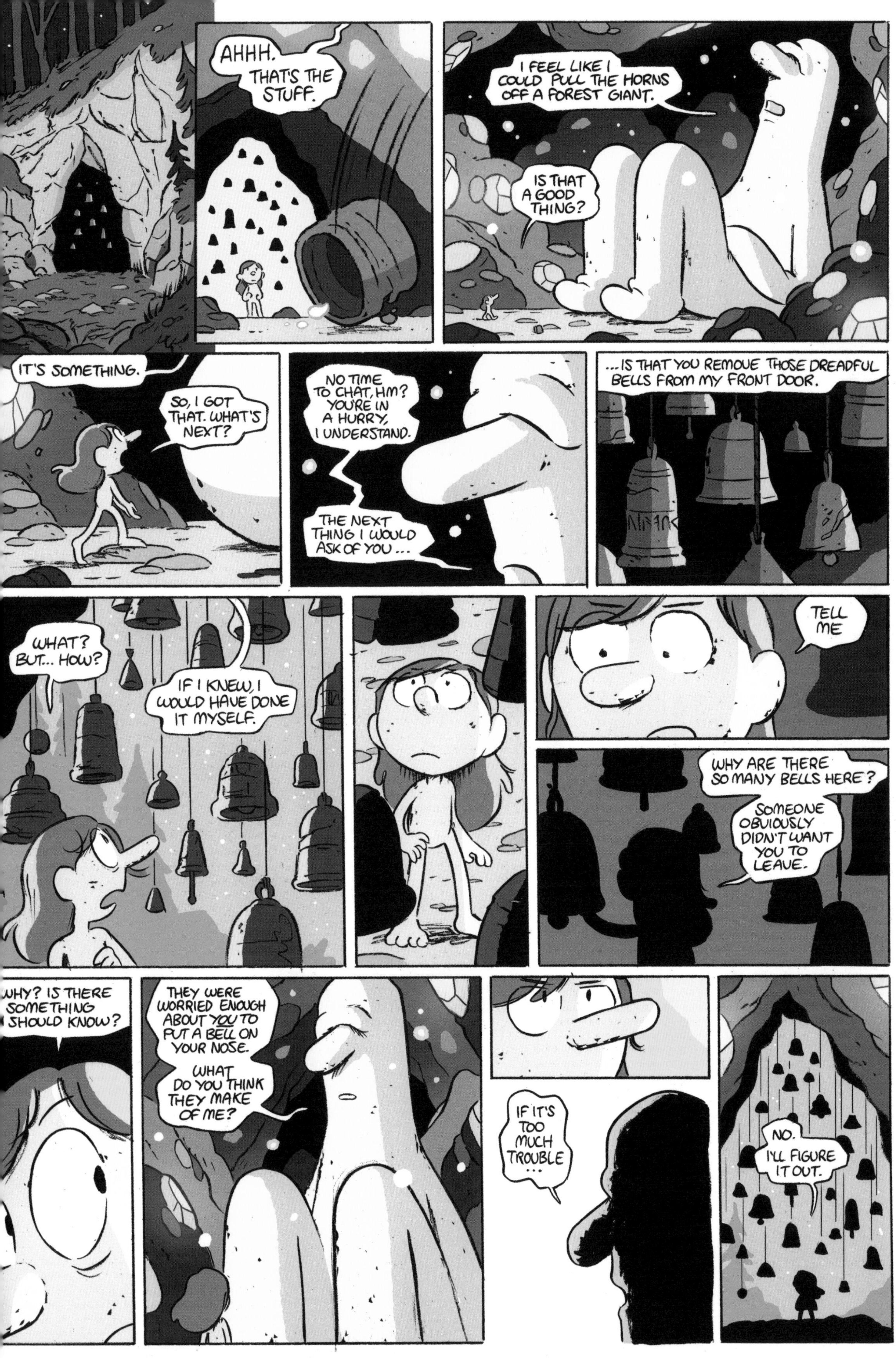

AHHH.
THAT'S THE STUFF.
I FEEL LIKE I COULD PULL THE HORNS OFF A FOREST GIANT.
IS THAT A GOOD THING?
IT'S SOMETHING.
SO, I GOT THAT. WHAT'S NEXT?
NO TIME TO CHAT, HM? YOU'RE IN A HURRY, I UNDERSTAND.
THE NEXT THING I WOULD ASK OF YOU ...
...IS THAT YOU REMOVE THOSE DREADFUL BELLS FROM MY FRONT DOOR.
WHAT? BUT... HOW?
IF I KNEW, I WOULD HAVE DONE IT MYSELF.
TELL ME
WHY ARE THERE SO MANY BELLS HERE?
SOMEONE OBVIOUSLY DIDN'T WANT YOU TO LEAVE.
WHY? IS THERE SOMETHING SHOULD KNOW?
THEY WERE WORRIED ENOUGH ABOUT YOU TO PUT A BELL ON YOUR NOSE.
WHAT DO YOU THINK THEY MAKE OF ME?
IF IT'S TOO MUCH TROUBLE ...
NO. I'LL FIGURE IT OUT.

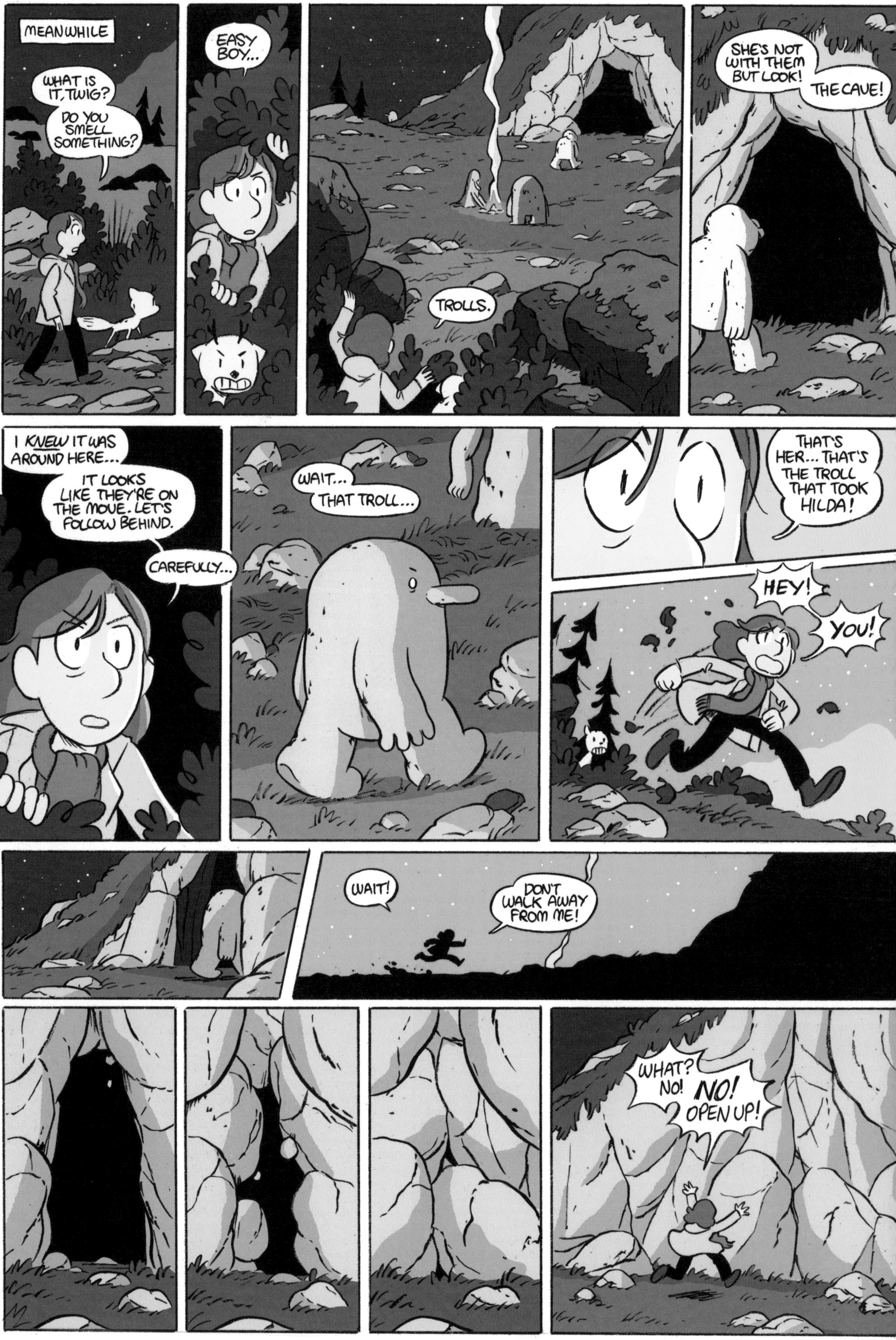
MEANWHILE
WHAT IS IT, TWIG?
DO YOU SMELL SOMETHING?
EASY BOY...
TROLLS.
SHE'S NOT WITH THEM BUT LOOK!
THE CAVE!
I KNEW IT WAS AROUND HERE...
IT LOOKS LIKE THEY'RE ON THE MOVE. LET'S FOLLOW BEHIND.
CAREFULLY...
WAIT...
THAT TROLL...
THAT'S HER... THAT'S THE TROLL THAT TOOK HILDA!
HEY!
YOU!
WAIT!
DON'T WALK AWAY FROM ME!
WHAT? NO!
NO!
OPEN UP!

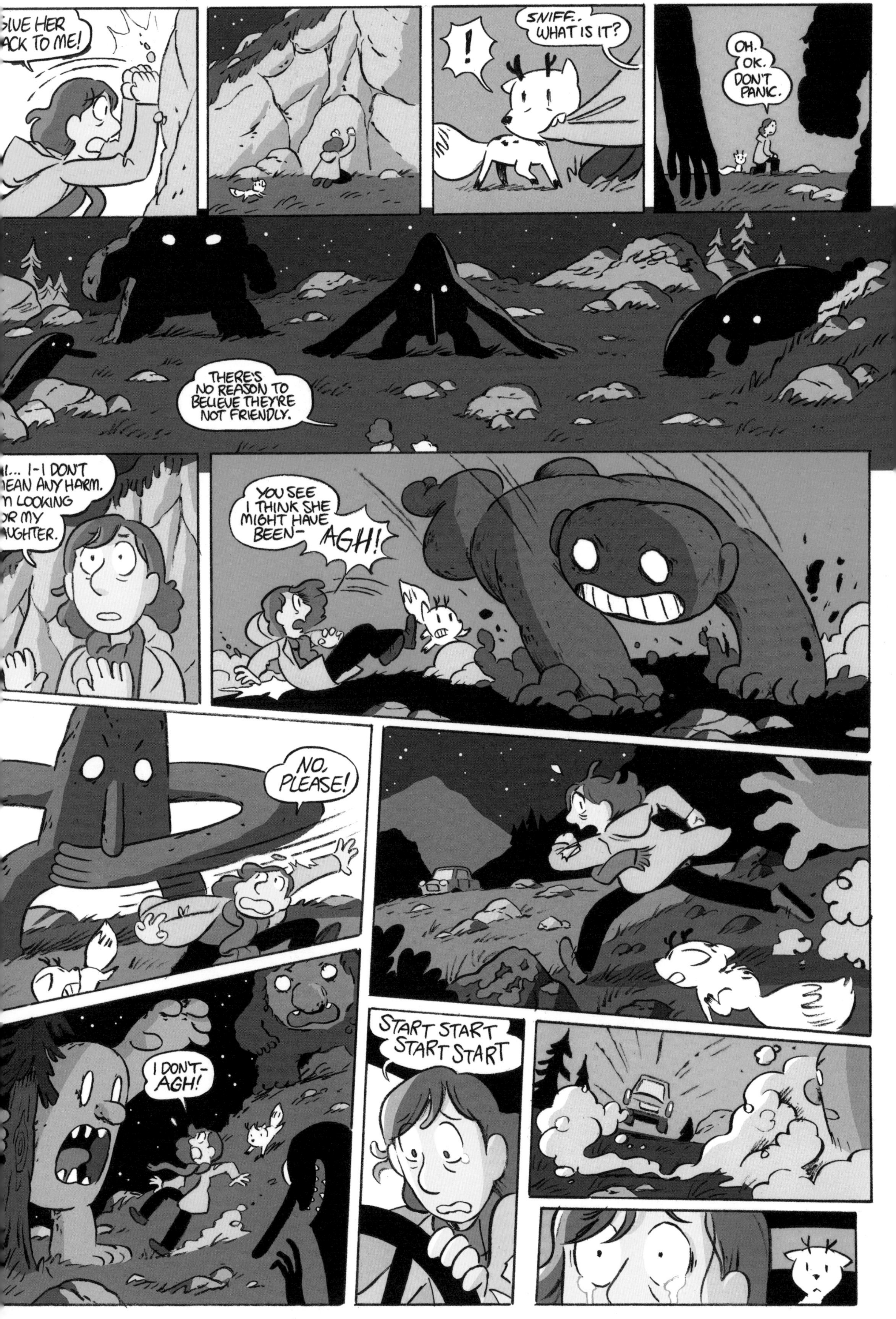

GIVE HER
BACK TO ME!
!
SNIFF.. WHAT IS IT?
OH. OK. DON'T PANIC.
THERE'S NO REASON TO BELIEVE THEY'RE NOT FRIENDLY.
I-I DON'T
MEAN ANY HARM.
LOOKING
FOR MY
DAUGHTER.
YOU SEE I THINK SHE MIGHT HAVE BEEN-
AGH!
NO, PLEASE!
I DON'T-
AGH!
START START START START

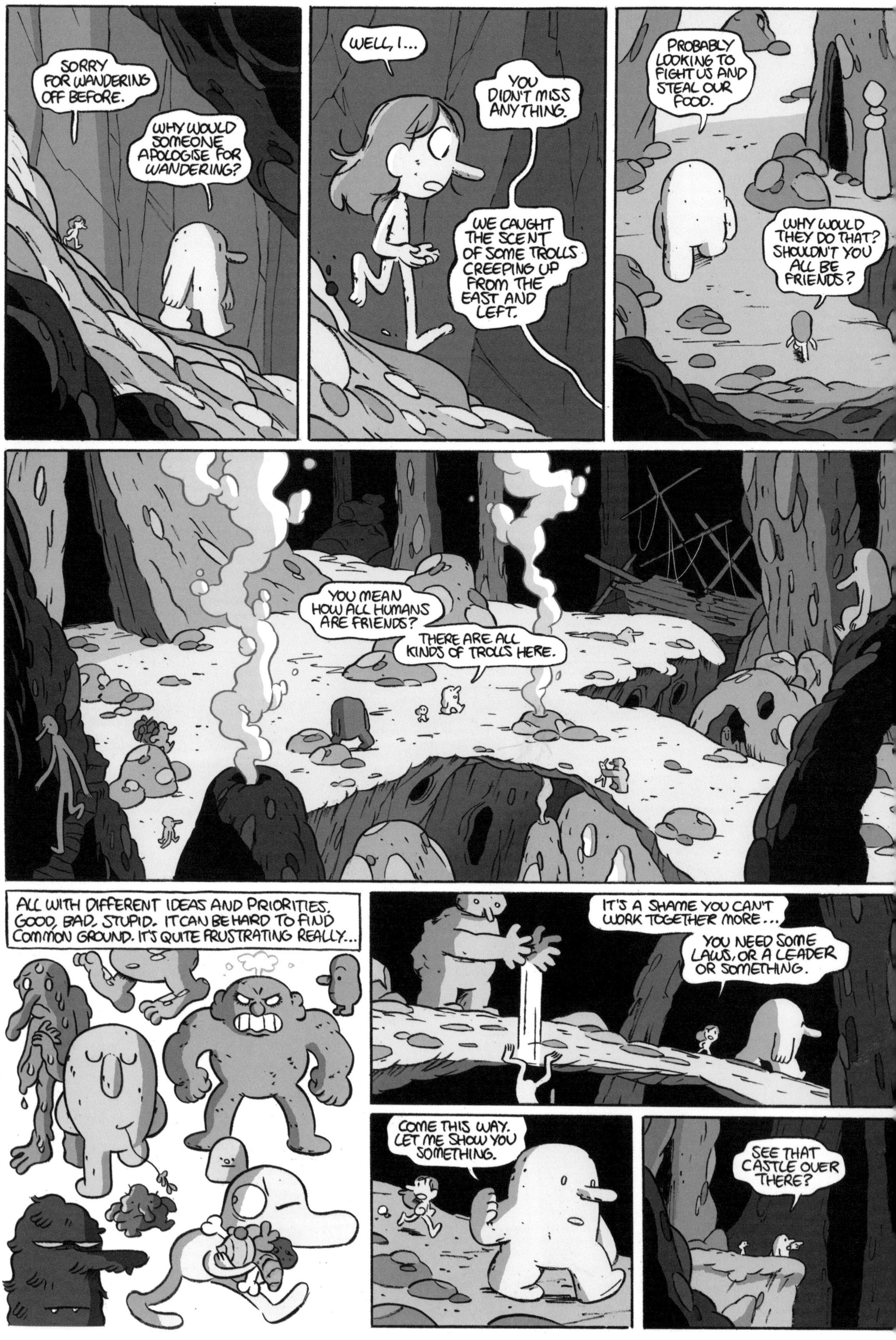
SORRY FOR WANDERING OFF BEFORE.
WHY WOULD SOMEONE APOLOGISE FOR WANDERING?
WELL, I...
YOU DIDN'T MISS ANYTHING.
WE CAUGHT THE SCENT OF SOME TROLLS CREEPING UP FROM THE EAST AND LEFT.
PROBABLY LOOKING TO FIGHT US AND STEAL OUR FOOD.
WHY WOULD THEY DO THAT? SHOULDN'T YOU ALL BE FRIENDS?
YOU MEAN HOW ALL HUMANS ARE FRIENDS?
THERE ARE ALL KINDS OF TROLLS HERE.
ALL WITH DIFFERENT IDEAS AND PRIORITIES. GOOD, BAD, STUPID. IT CAN BE HARD TO FIND COMMON GROUND. IT'S QUITE FRUSTRATING REALLY...
IT'S A SHAME YOU CAN'T WORK TOGETHER MORE...
YOU NEED SOME LAWS, OR A LEADER OR SOMETHING.
COME THIS WAY. LET ME SHOW YOU SOMETHING.
SEE THAT CASTLE OVER THERE?

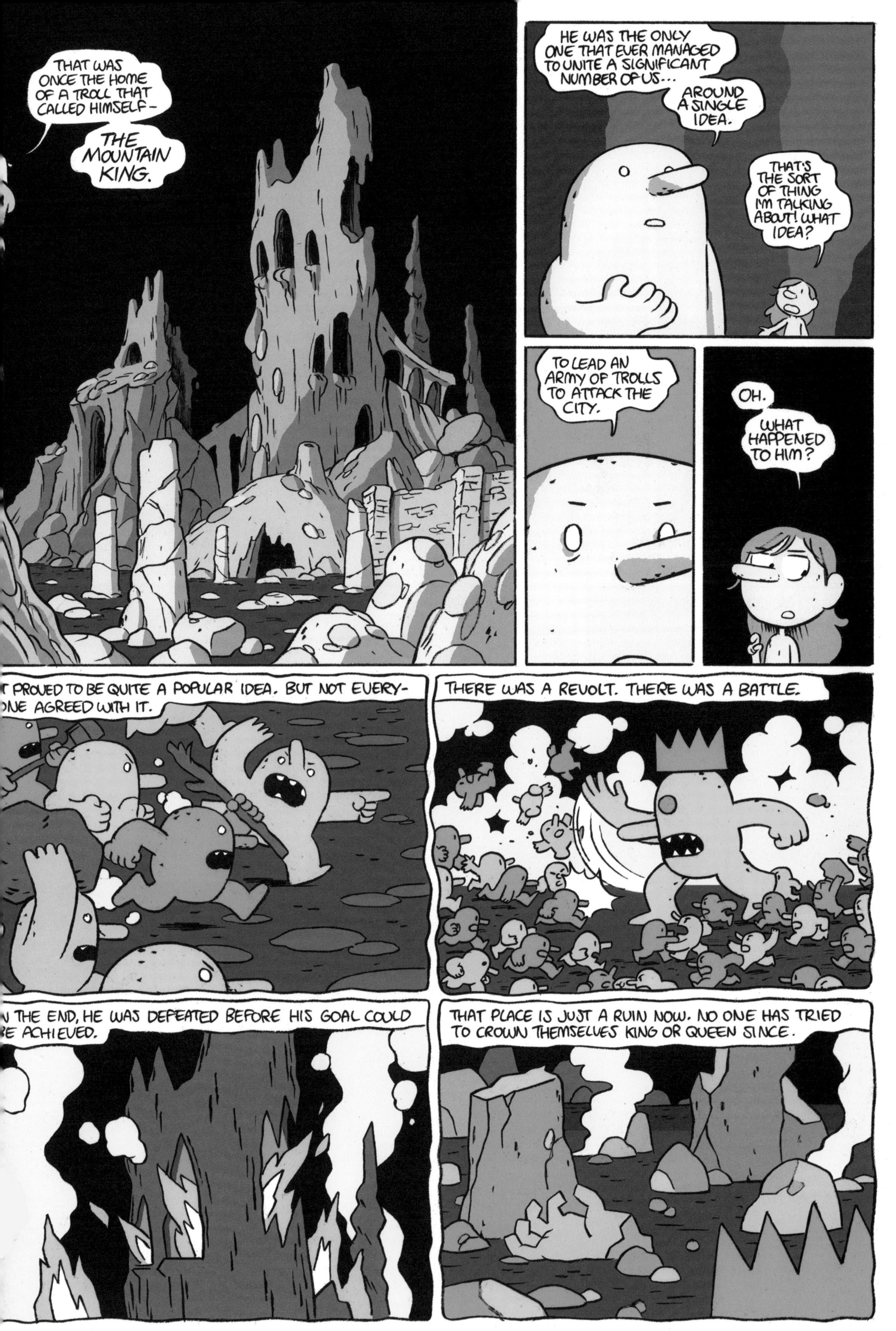
THAT WAS ONCE THE HOME OF A TROLL THAT CALLED HIMSELF-
THE MOUNTAIN KING.
HE WAS THE ONLY ONE THAT EVER MANAGED TO UNITE A SIGNIFICANT NUMBER OF US...
AROUND A SINGLE IDEA.
THAT'S THE SORT OF THING I'M TALKING ABOUT! WHAT IDEA?
TO LEAD AN ARMY OF TROLLS TO ATTACK THE CITY.
OH.
WHAT HAPPENED TO HIM?
T PROVED TO BE QUITE A POPULAR IDEA. BUT NOT EVERY-
ONE AGREED WITH IT.
THERE WAS A REVOLT. THERE WAS A BATTLE.
N THE END, HE WAS DEFEATED BEFORE HIS GOAL COULD
E ACHIEVED.
THAT PLACE IS JUST A RUIN NOW. NO ONE HAS TRIED TO CROWN THEMSELVES KING OR QUEEN SINCE.

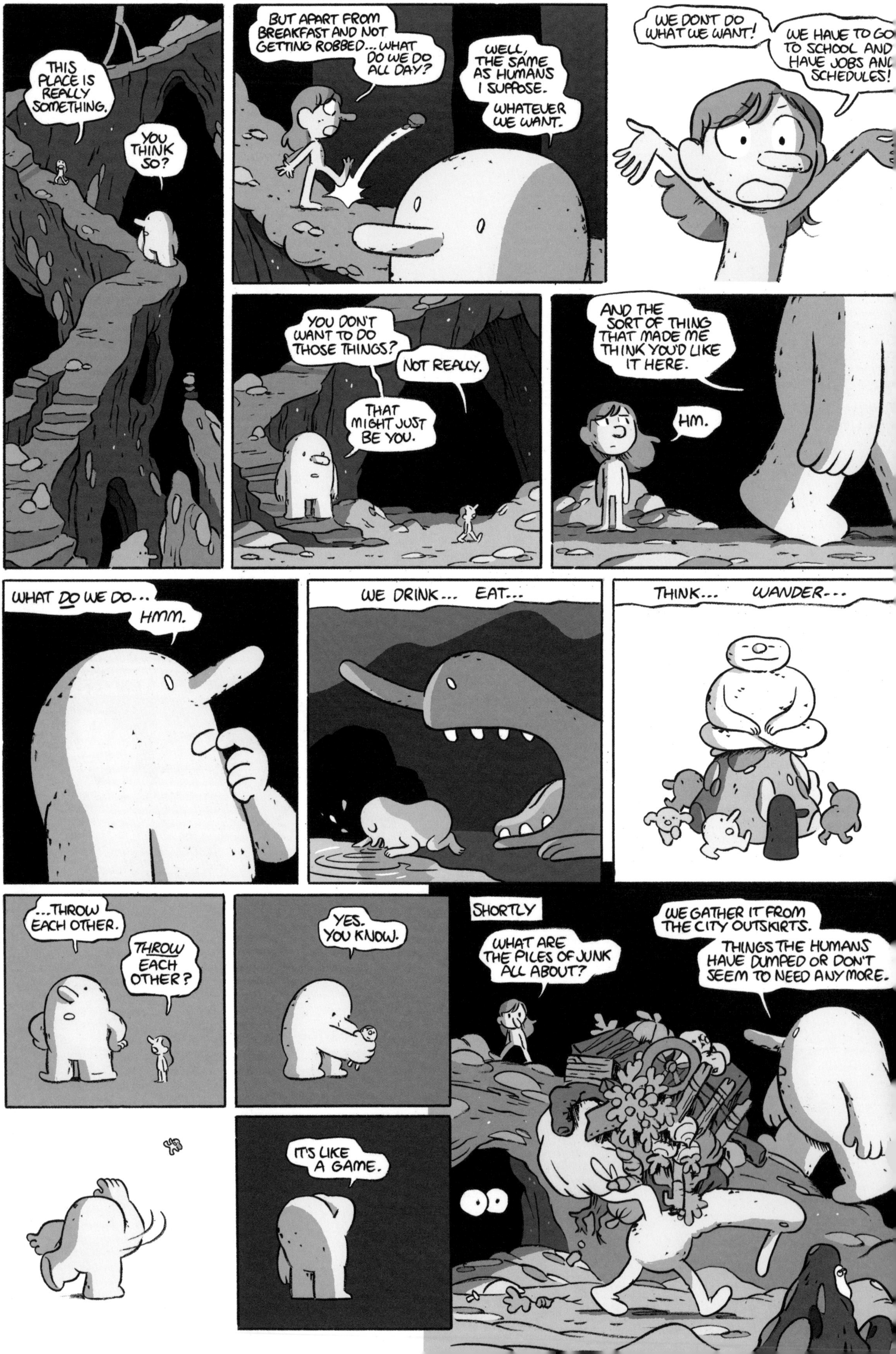
THIS PLACE IS REALLY SOMETHING.
YOU THINK SO?
BUT APART FROM BREAKFAST AND NOT GETTING ROBBED... WHAT DO WE DO ALL DAY?
WELL, THE SAME AS HUMANS I SUPPOSE.
WHATEVER WE WANT.
WE DONT DO WHAT WE WANT!
WE HAVE TO GO TO SCHOOL AND HAVE JOBS AND SCHEDULES!
YOU DON'T WANT TO DO THOSE THINGS?
NOT REALLY.
THAT MIGHT JUST BE YOU.
AND THE SORT OF THING THAT MADE ME THINK YOU'D LIKE IT HERE.
HM.
WHAT DO WE DO...
HMM.
WE DRINK... EAT...
THINK... WANDER...
...THROW EACH OTHER.
THROW EACH OTHER?
YES. YOU KNOW.
IT'S LIKE A GAME.
SHORTLY
WHAT ARE THE PILES OF JUNK ALL ABOUT?
WE GATHER IT FROM THE CITY OUTSKIRTS.
THINGS THE HUMANS HAVE DUMPED OR DON'T SEEM TO NEED ANYMORE.

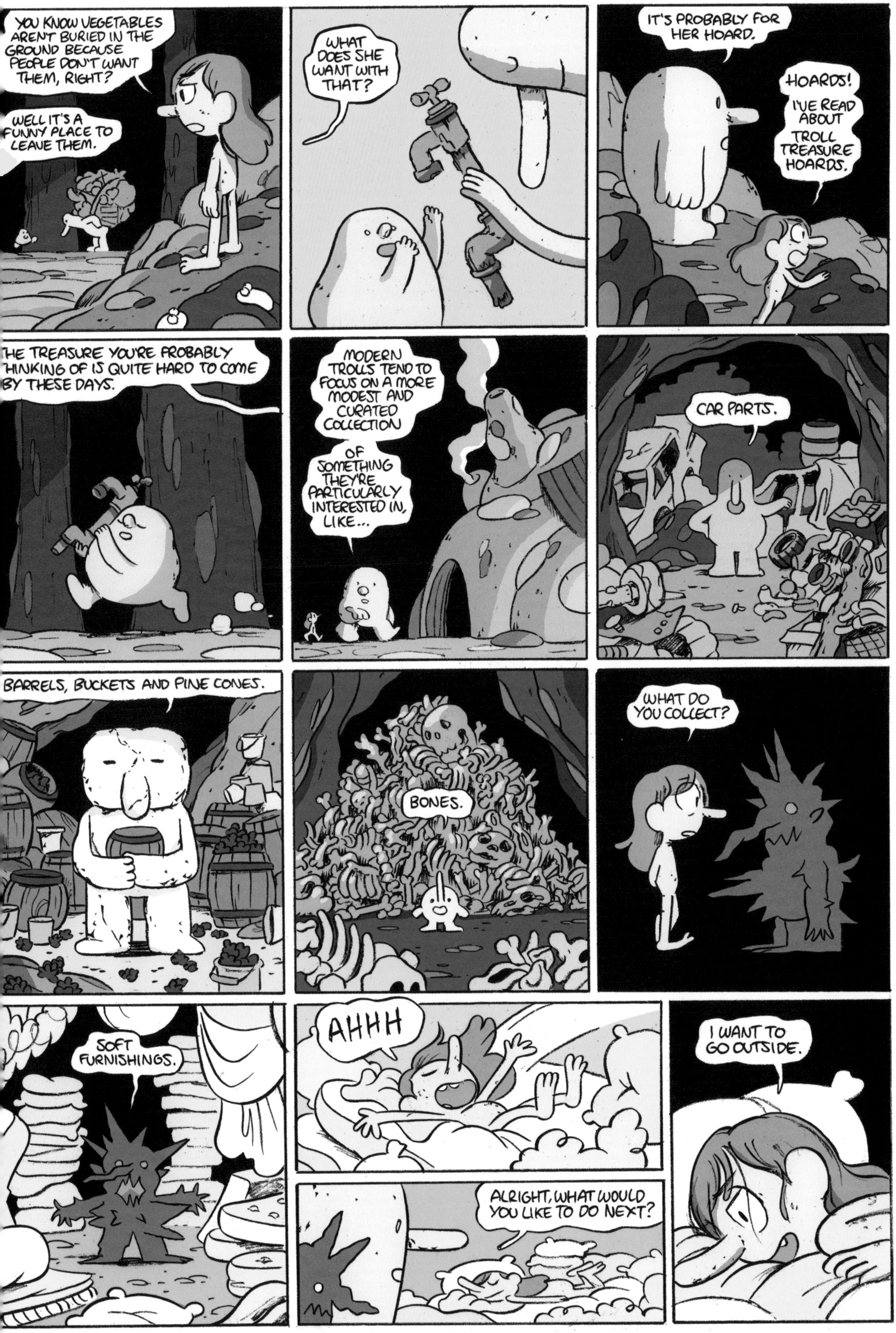
YOU KNOW VEGETABLES AREN'T BURIED IN THE GROUND BECAUSE PEOPLE DON'T WANT THEM, RIGHT?
WELL IT'S A FUNNY PLACE TO LEAVE THEM.
WHAT DOES SHE WANT WITH THAT?
IT'S PROBABLY FOR HER HOARD.
HOARDS!
I'VE READ ABOUT TROLL TREASURE HOARDS.
THE TREASURE YOU'RE PROBABLY THINKING OF IS QUITE HARD TO COME BY THESE DAYS.
MODERN TROLLS TEND TO FOCUS ON A MORE MODEST AND CURATED COLLECTION
OF SOMETHING THEY'RE PARTICULARLY INTERESTED IN, LIKE...
CAR PARTS.
BARRELS, BUCKETS AND PINE CONES.
BONES.
WHAT DO YOU COLLECT?
SOFT FURNISHINGS.
AHHH
ALRIGHT, WHAT WOULD YOU LIKE TO DO NEXT?
I WANT TO GO OUTSIDE.

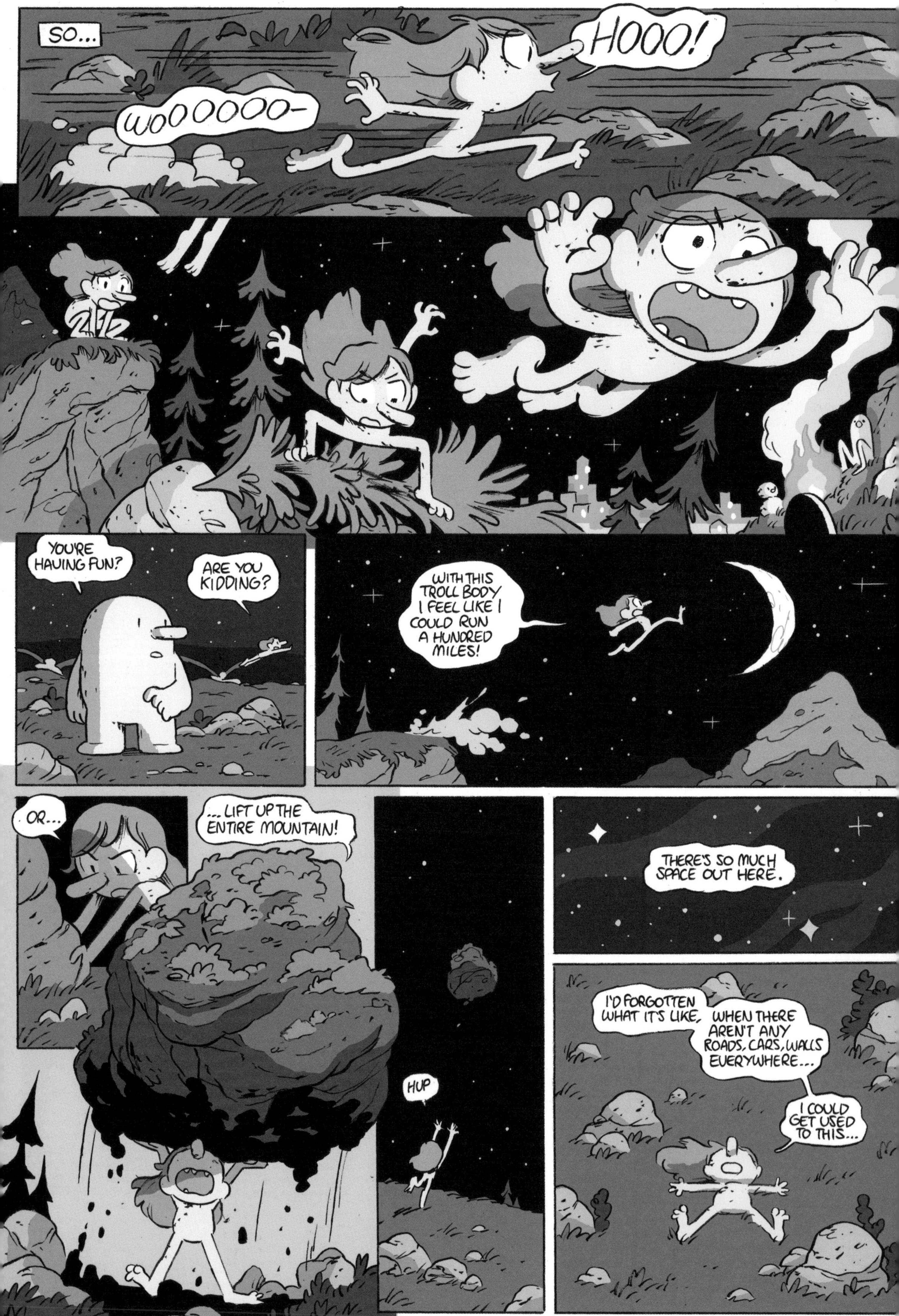
SO...
HOOO!
WOOOOOO-
YOU'RE HAVING FUN?
ARE YOU KIDDING?
WITH THIS TROLL BODY I FEEL LIKE I COULD RUN A HUNDRED MILES!
OR...
...LIFT UP THE ENTIRE MOUNTAIN!
HUP
THERE'S SO MUCH SPACE OUT HERE.
I'D FORGOTTEN WHAT IT'S LIKE,
WHEN THERE AREN'T ANY ROADS, CARS, WALLS EVERYWHERE...
I COULD GET USED TO THIS...

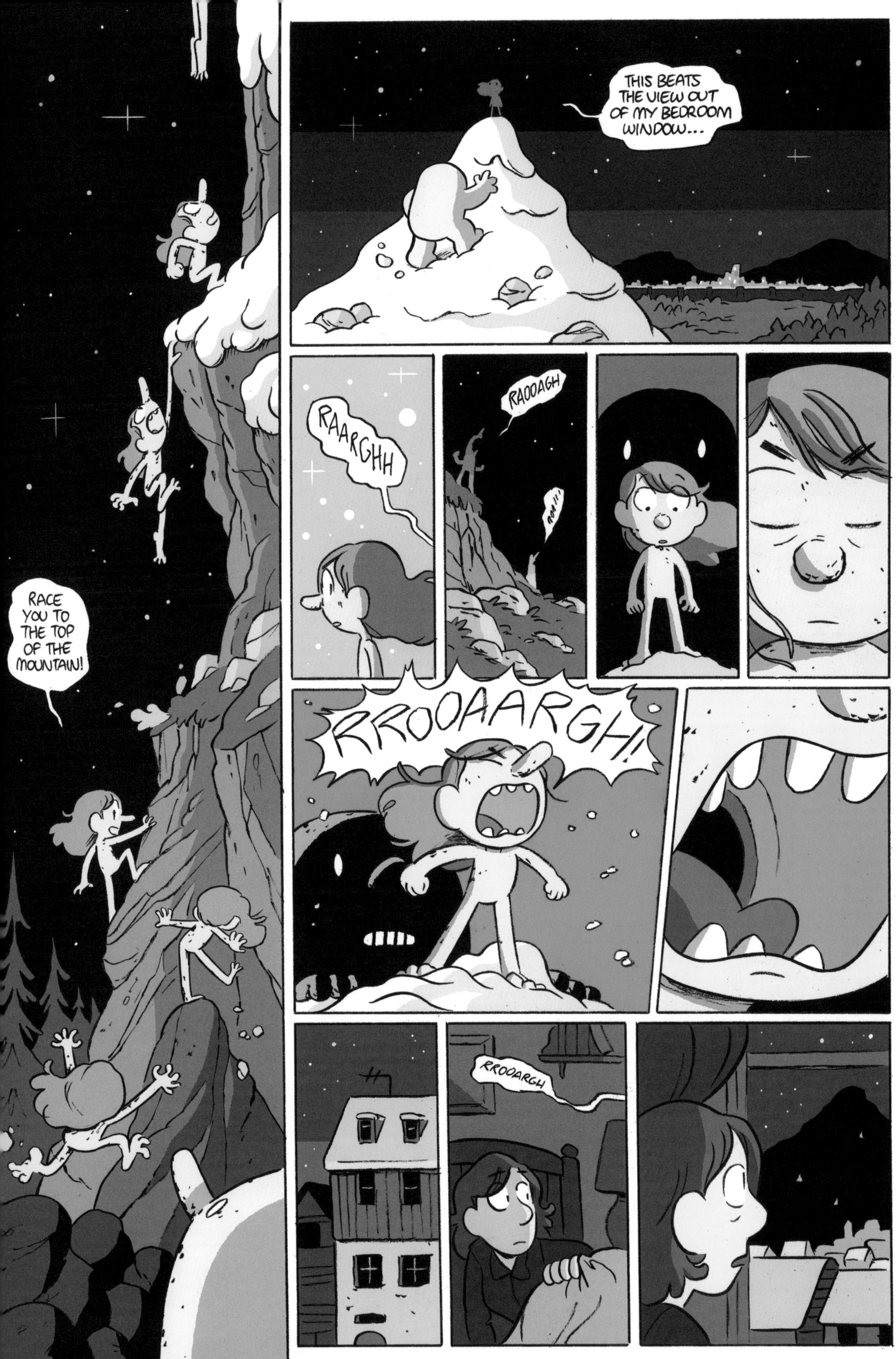
RACE YOU TO THE TOP OF THE MOUNTAIN!
THIS BEATS THE VIEW OUT OF MY BEDROOM WINDOW...
RAARGHH
RAOOAGH
RRROOAARGH!
RROOARGH

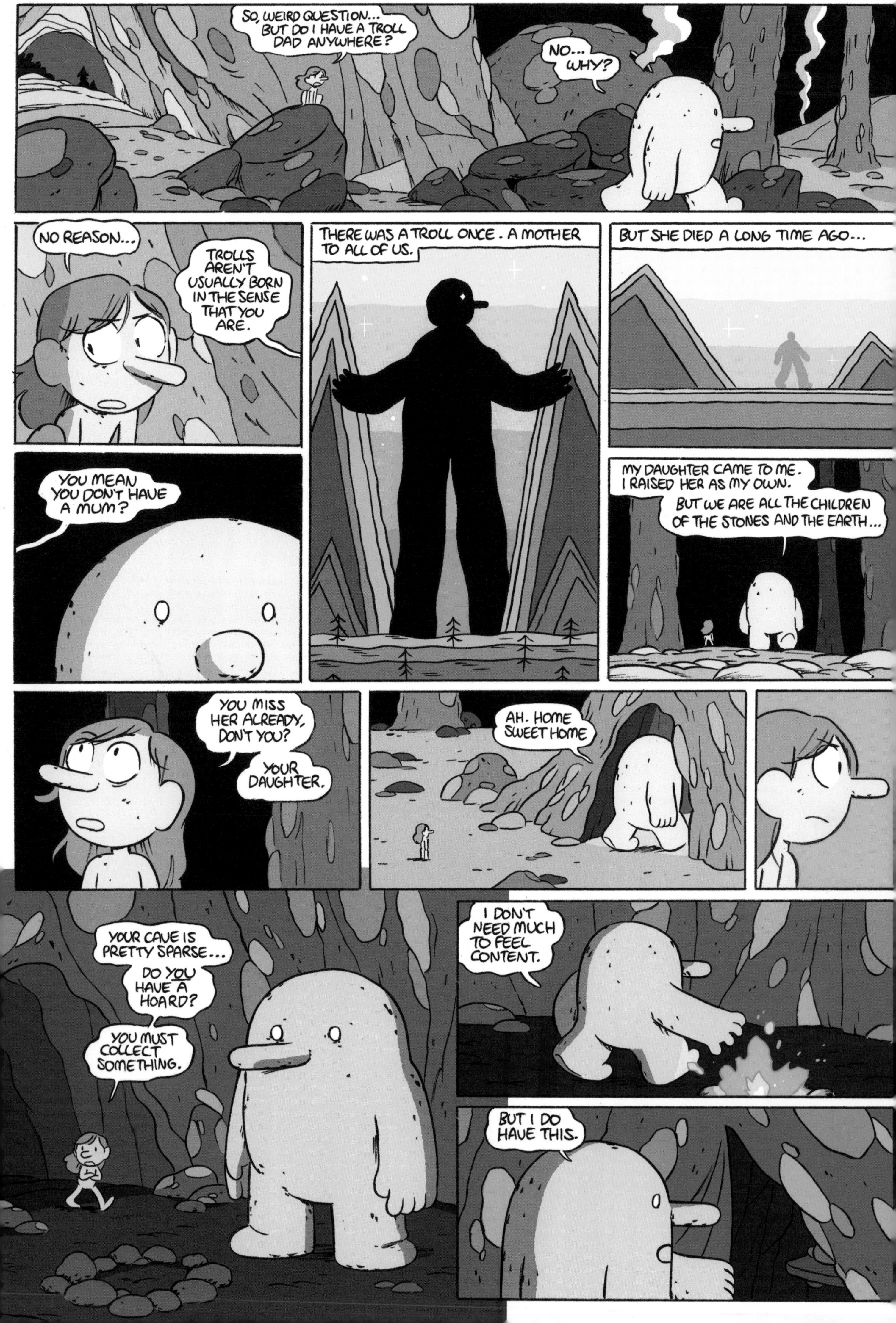
SO, WEIRD QUESTION... BUT DO I HAVE A TROLL DAD ANYWHERE?
NO... WHY?
NO REASON...
TROLLS AREN'T USUALLY BORN IN THE SENSE THAT YOU ARE.
THERE WAS A TROLL ONCE. A MOTHER TO ALL OF US.
BUT SHE DIED A LONG TIME AGO...
YOU MEAN YOU DON'T HAVE A MUM?
MY DAUGHTER CAME TO ME. I RAISED HER AS MY OWN.
BUT WE ARE ALL THE CHILDREN OF THE STONES AND THE EARTH...
YOU MISS HER ALREADY, DON'T YOU?
YOUR DAUGHTER.
AH. HOME SWEET HOME
YOUR CAVE IS PRETTY SPARSE...
DO YOU HAVE A HOARD?
YOU MUST COLLECT SOMETHING.
I DON'T NEED MUCH TO FEEL CONTENT.
BUT I DO HAVE THIS.

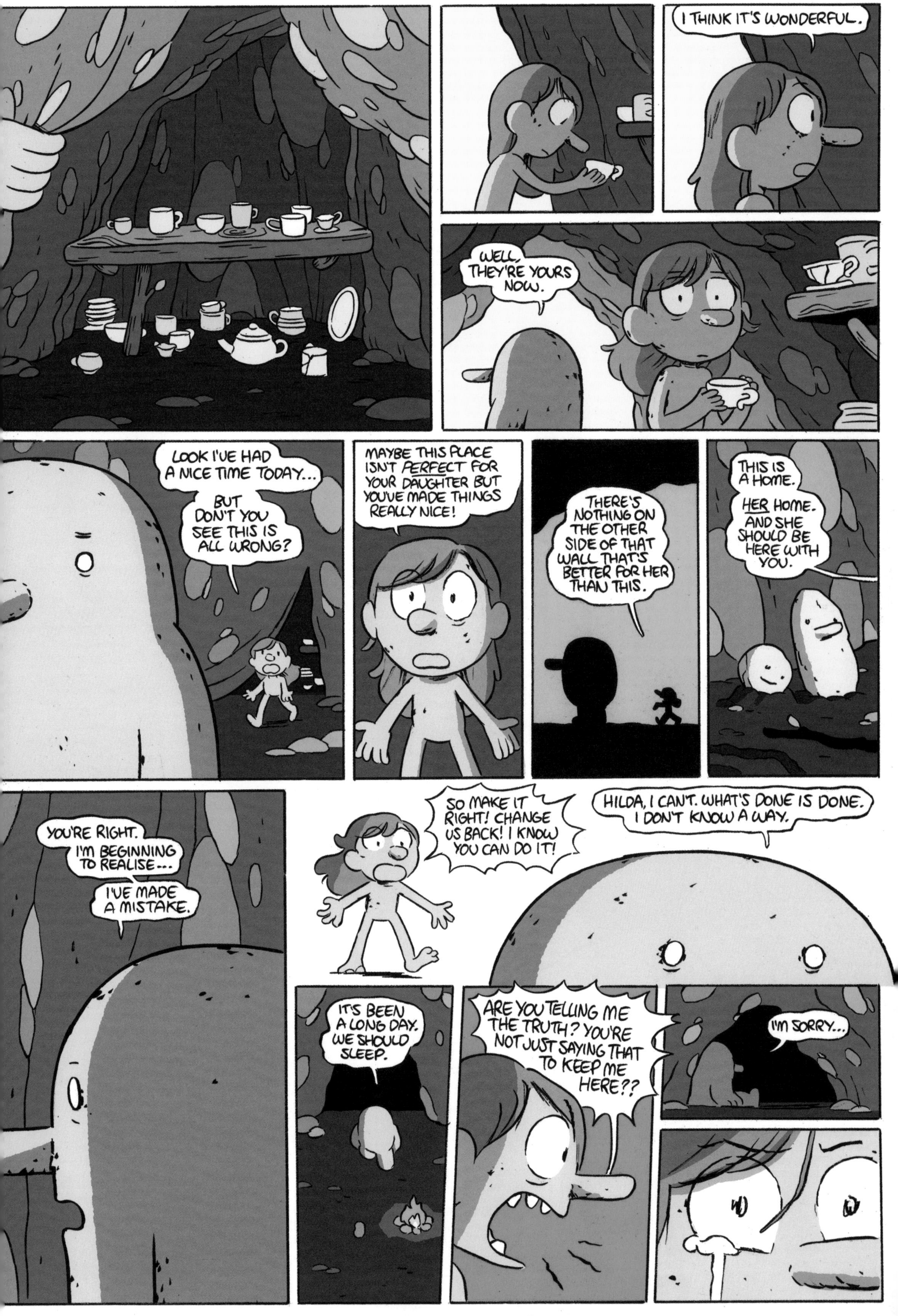

I THINK IT'S WONDERFUL.
WELL, THEY'RE YOURS NOW.
LOOK I'VE HAD A NICE TIME TODAY...
BUT DON'T YOU SEE THIS IS ALL WRONG?
MAYBE THIS PLACE ISN'T PERFECT FOR YOUR DAUGHTER BUT YOU'VE MADE THINGS REALLY NICE!
THERE'S NOTHING ON THE OTHER SIDE OF THAT WALL THAT'S BETTER FOR HER THAN THIS.
THIS IS A HOME.
HER HOME. AND SHE SHOULD BE HERE WITH YOU.
YOU'RE RIGHT. I'M BEGINNING TO REALISE...
I'VE MADE A MISTAKE.
SO MAKE IT RIGHT! CHANGE US BACK! I KNOW YOU CAN DO IT!
HILDA, I CAN'T. WHAT'S DONE IS DONE. I DON'T KNOW A WAY.
IT'S BEEN A LONG DAY. WE SHOULD SLEEP.
ARE YOU TELLING ME THE TRUTH? YOU'RE NOT JUST SAYING THAT TO KEEP ME HERE??
I'M SORRY...

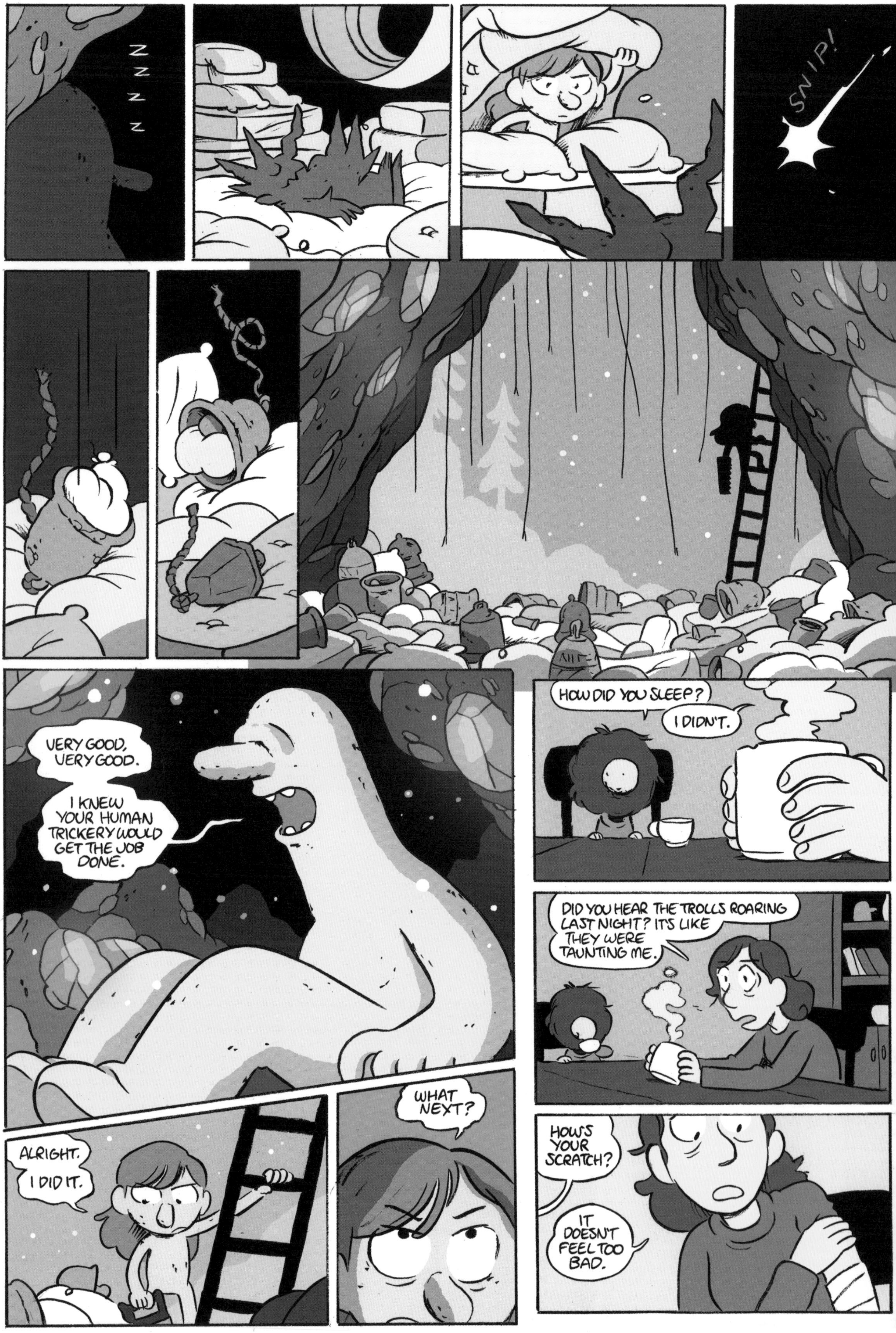
Z Z Z Z
SNIP!
VERY GOOD, VERY GOOD.
I KNEW YOUR HUMAN TRICKERY WOULD GET THE JOB DONE.
HOW DID YOU SLEEP?
I DIDN'T.
DID YOU HEAR THE TROLLS ROARING LAST NIGHT? IT'S LIKE THEY WERE TAUNTING ME.
ALRIGHT.
I DID IT.
WHAT NEXT?
HOW'S YOUR SCRATCH?
IT DOESN'T FEEL TOO BAD.

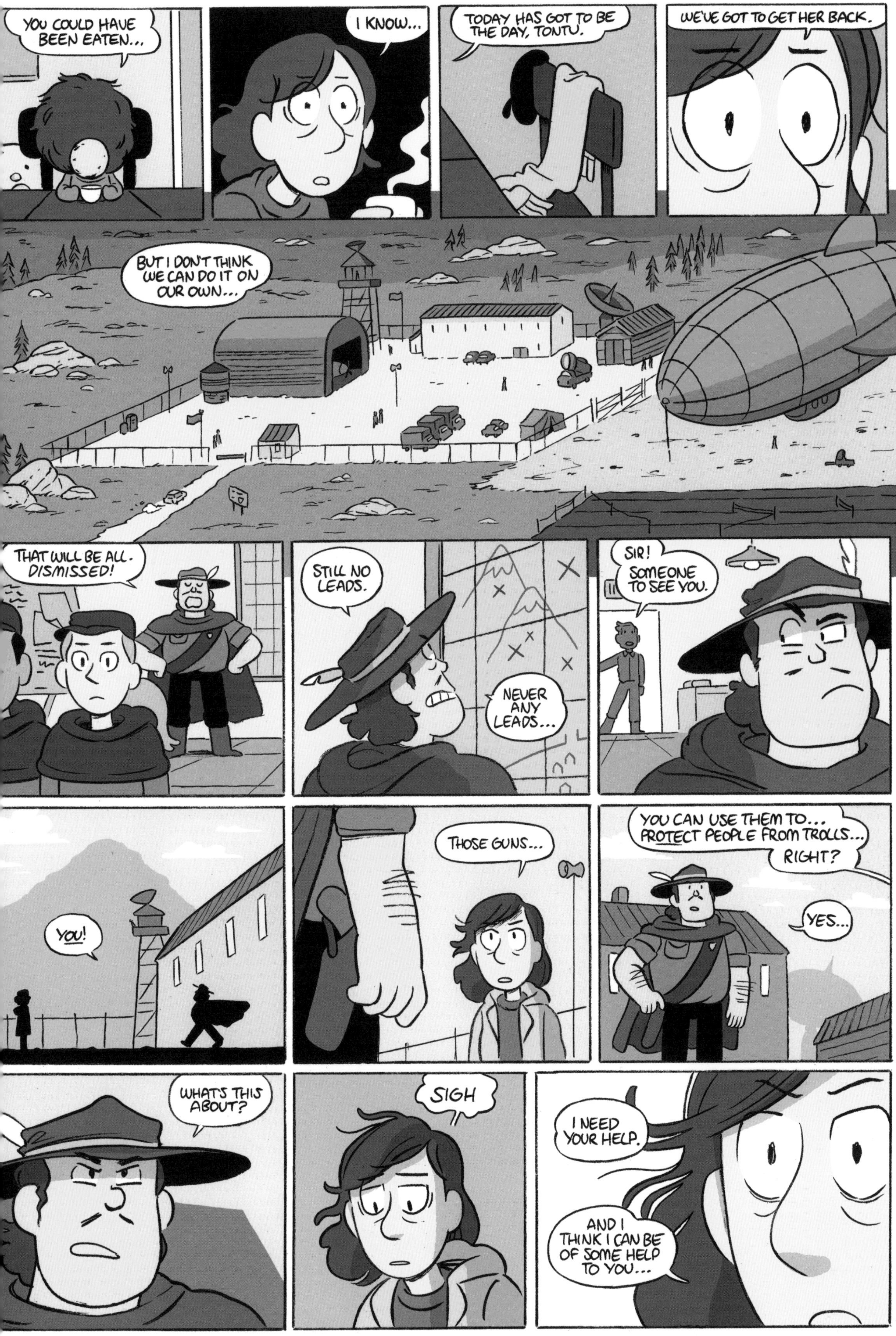

YOU COULD HAVE BEEN EATEN...
I KNOW...
TODAY HAS GOT TO BE THE DAY, TONTU.
WE'VE GOT TO GET HER BACK.
BUT I DON'T THINK WE CAN DO IT ON OUR OWN...
THAT WILL BE ALL. DISMISSED!
STILL NO LEADS.
NEVER ANY LEADS...
SIR! SOMEONE TO SEE YOU.
YOU!
THOSE GUNS...
YOU CAN USE THEM TO... PROTECT PEOPLE FROM TROLLS... RIGHT?
YES...
WHAT'S THIS ABOUT?
SIGH
I NEED YOUR HELP.
AND I THINK I CAN BE OF SOME HELP TO YOU...

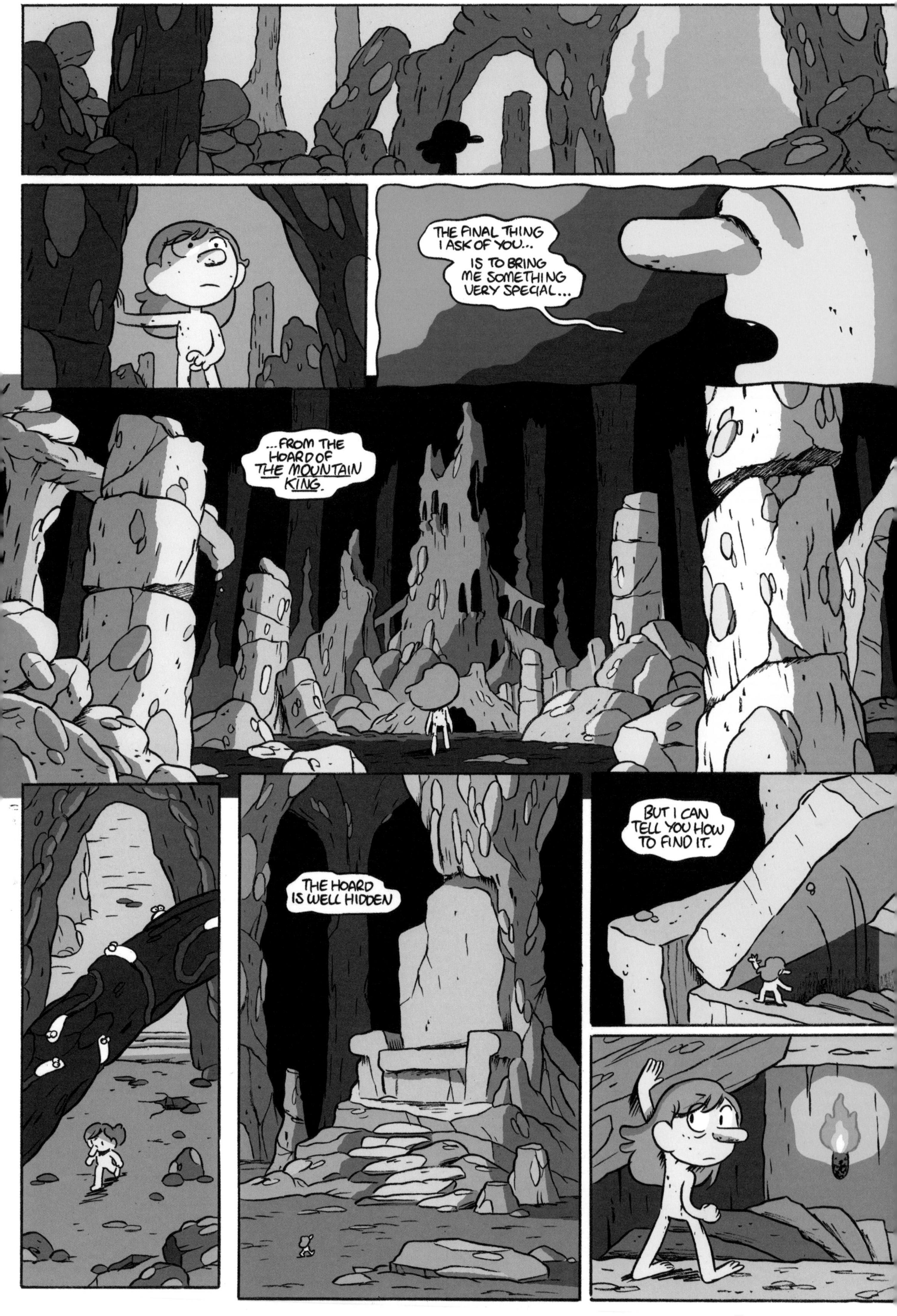
THE FINAL THING I ASK OF YOU... IS TO BRING ME SOMETHING VERY SPECIAL...
...FROM THE HOARD OF THE MOUNTAIN KING.
THE HOARD IS WELL HIDDEN
BUT I CAN TELL YOU HOW TO FIND IT.

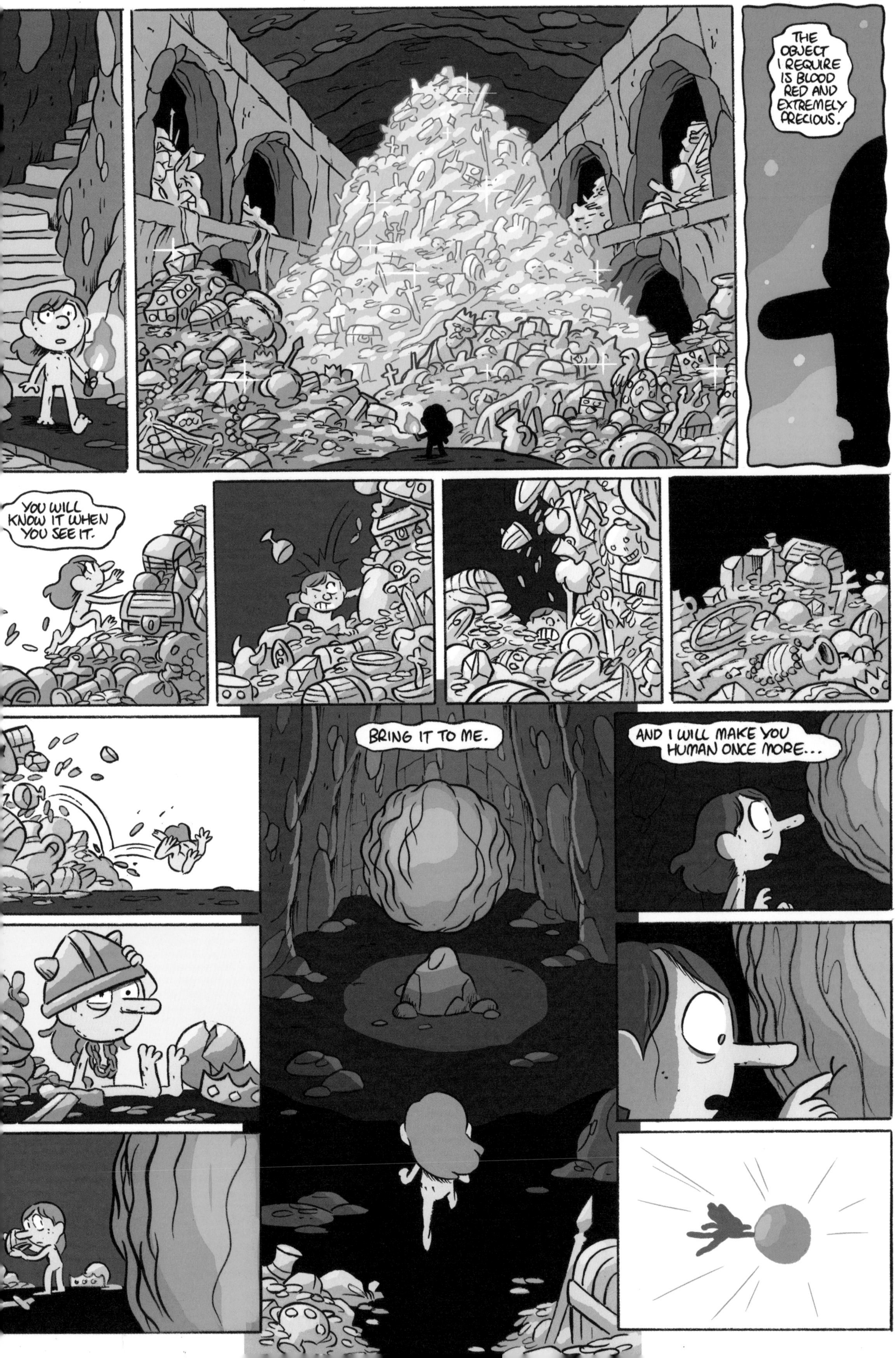
THE OBJECT I REQUIRE IS BLOOD RED AND EXTREMELY PRECIOUS.
YOU WILL KNOW IT WHEN YOU SEE IT.
BRING IT TO ME.
AND I WILL MAKE YOU HUMAN ONCE MORE...

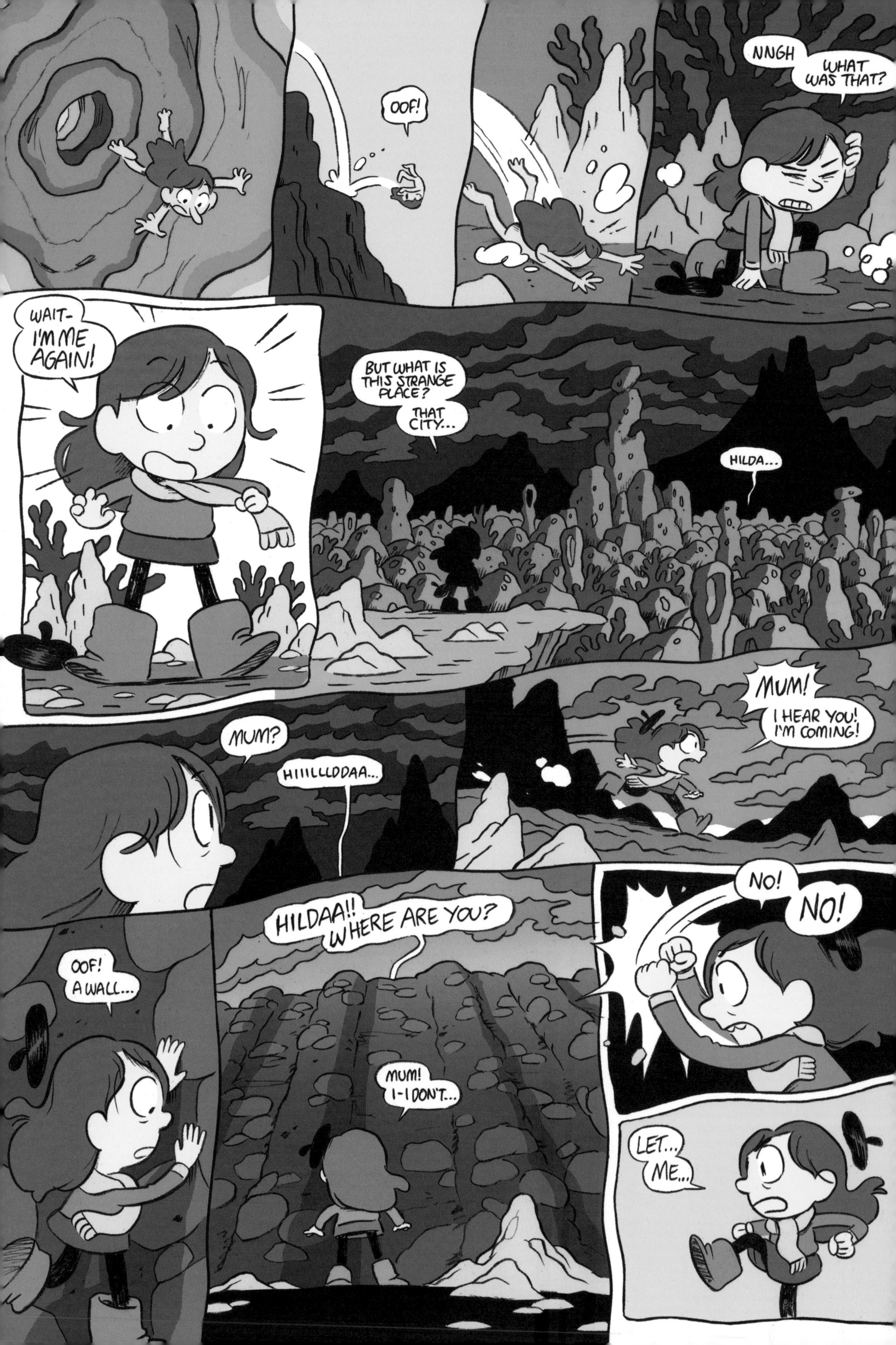
OOF!
NNGH
WHAT WAS THAT?
WAIT-
I'M ME AGAIN!
BUT WHAT IS THIS STRANGE PLACE?
THAT CITY...
HILDA...
MUM?
HIIILLLDDAA...
MUM!
I HEAR YOU! I'M COMING!
OOF! A WALL...
HILDAA!! WHERE ARE YOU?
MUM! I-I DON'T...
NO!
NO!
LET... ME...

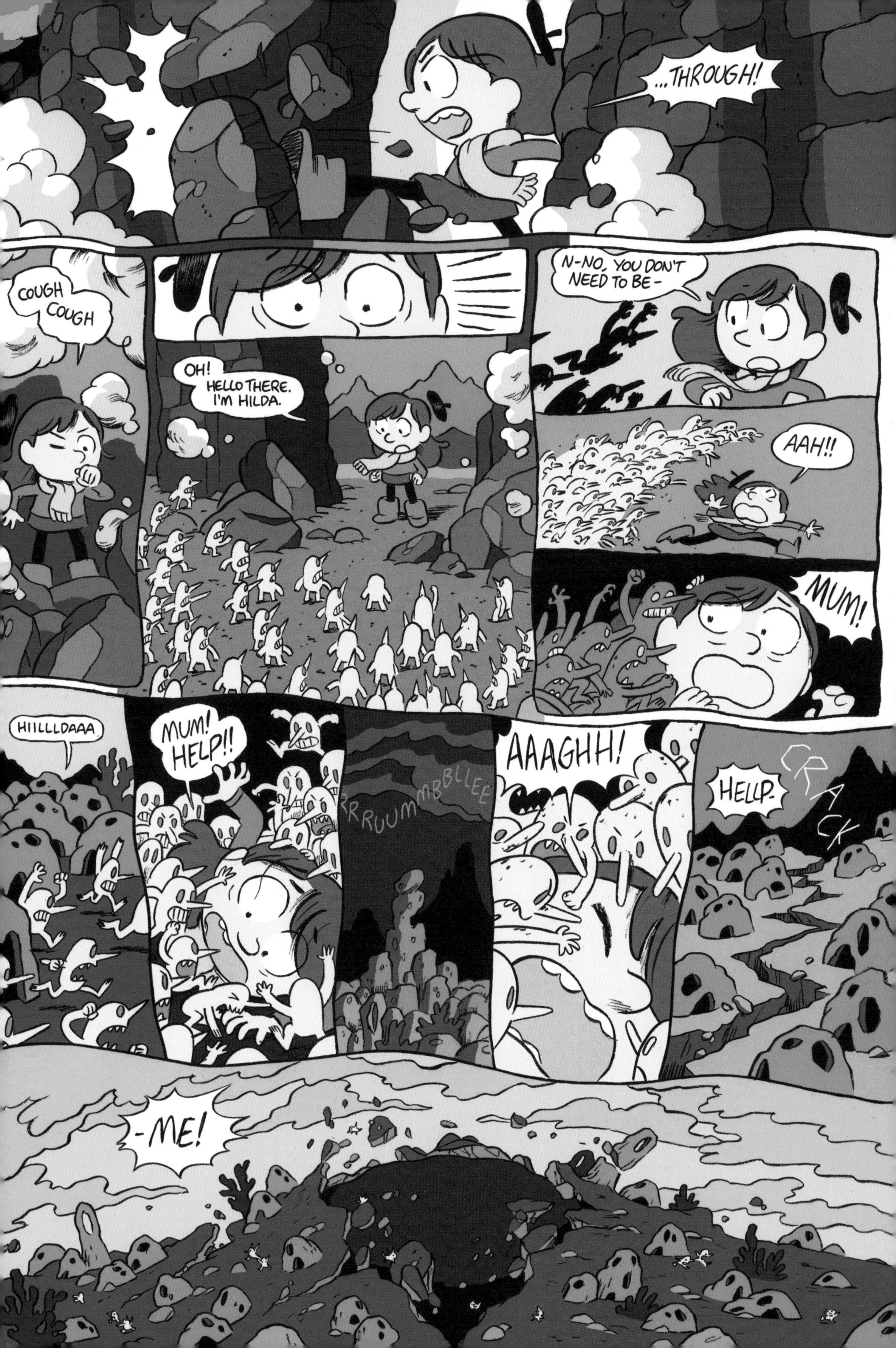
...THROUGH!
COUGH COUGH
OH! HELLO THERE. I'M HILDA.
N-NO, YOU DON'T NEED TO BE-
AAH!!
MUM!
HIILLLDAAA
MUM! HELP!!
RRRUUMMBBLLEE
AAAGHH!
HELLP-
CRACK
-ME!

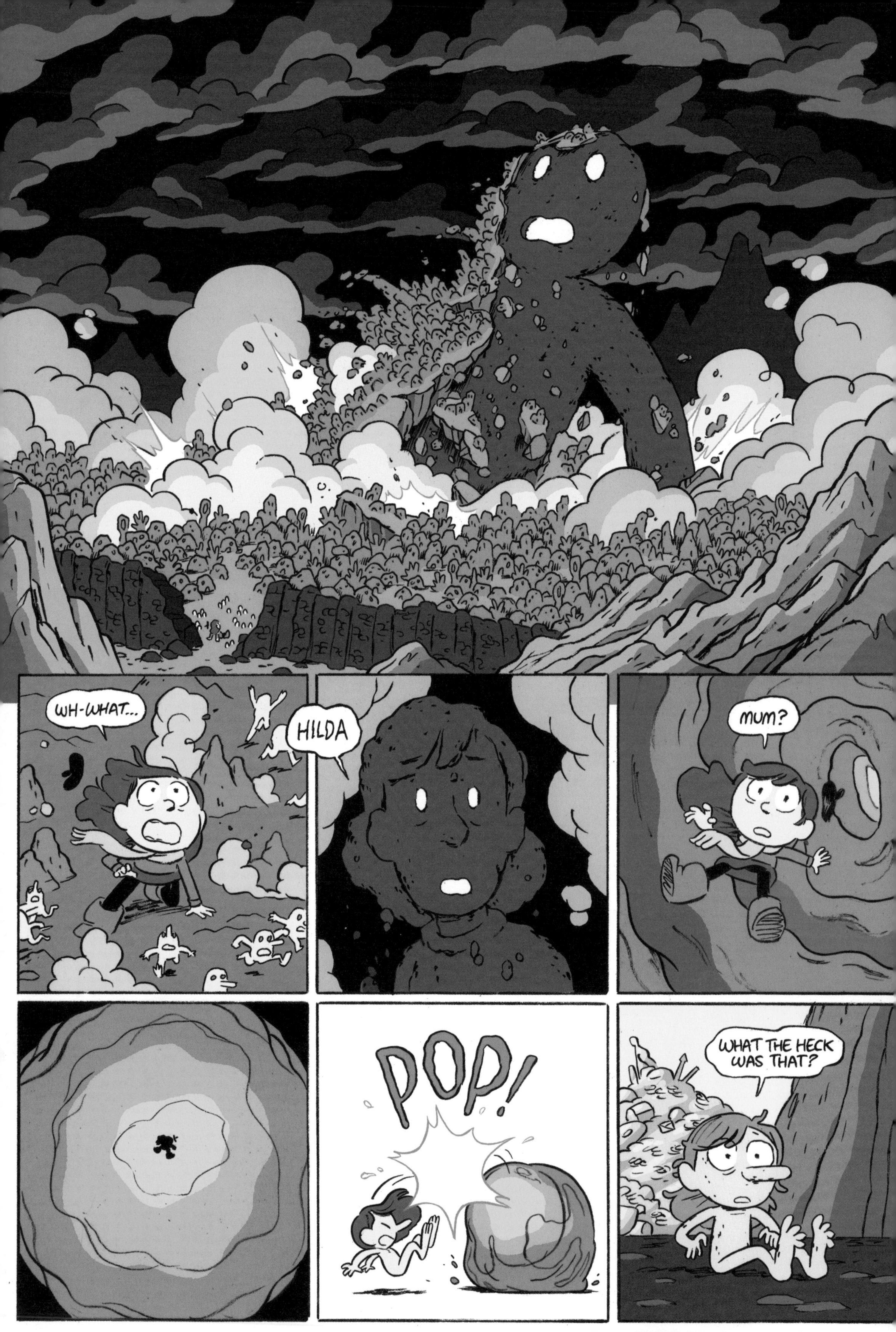

WH-WHAT...
HILDA
MUM?
POP!
WHAT THE HECK WAS THAT?

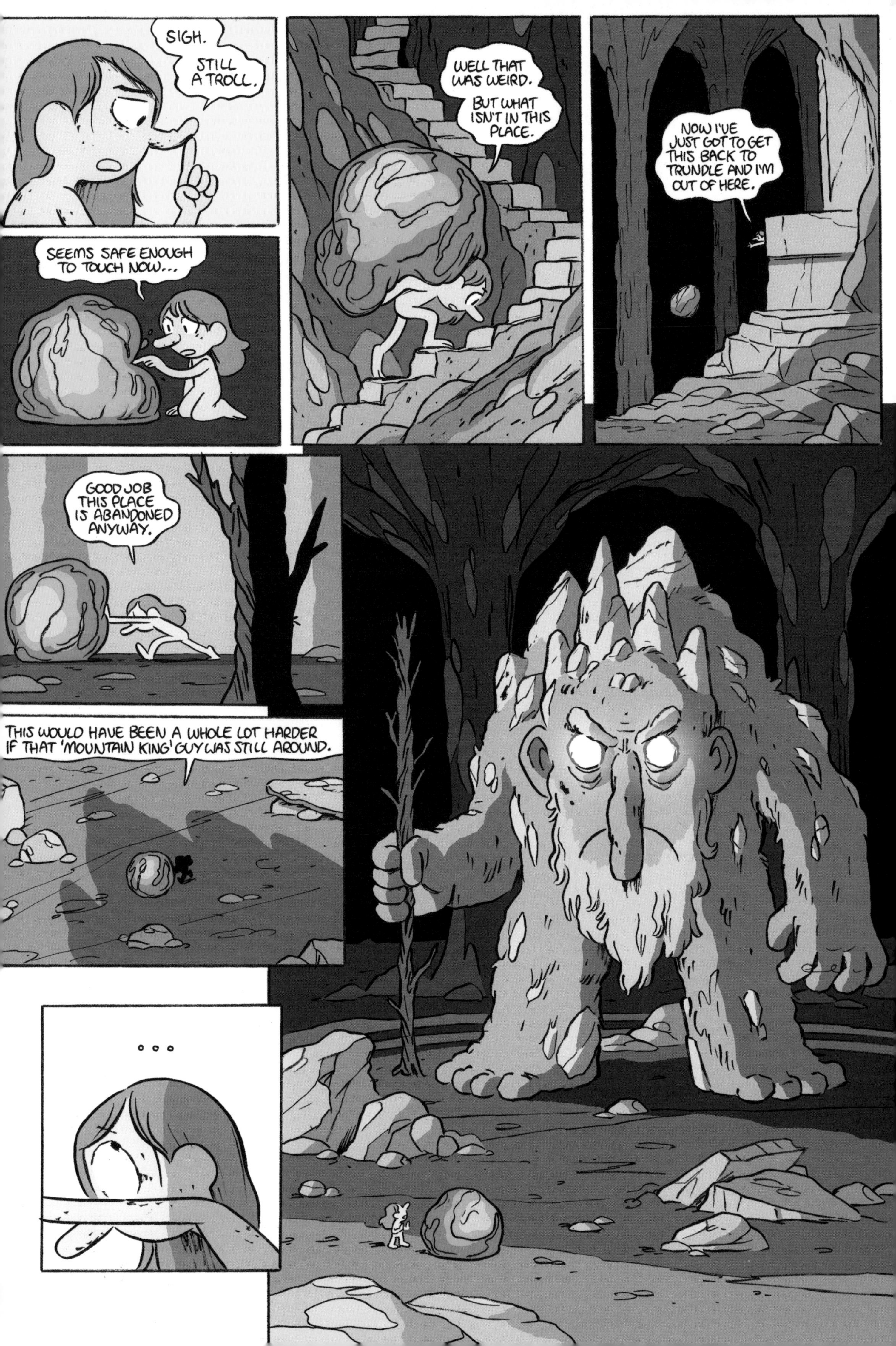
SIGH.
STILL A TROLL.
SEEMS SAFE ENOUGH TO TOUCH NOW...
WELL THAT WAS WEIRD.
BUT WHAT ISN'T IN THIS PLACE.
NOW I'VE JUST GOT TO GET THIS BACK TO TRUNDLE AND I'M OUT OF HERE.
GOOD JOB THIS PLACE IS ABANDONED ANYWAY.
THIS WOULD HAVE BEEN A WHOLE LOT HARDER IF THAT 'MOUNTAIN KING' GUY WAS STILL AROUND.
...

MEANWHILE

HA! THAT PUT THE FEAR OF DAY INTO THEM.

THIS IS THE PLACE.

HERE? BUT..WHERE'S THE CAVE?

IS THIS A JOKE?

IT'S NO SMALL MATTER YOU KNOW, DRAGGING ME OUT HERE AT THIS TIME OF NIGHT.

I'LL REMIND YOU THAT THE CONTINUED SAFETY OF TROLBERG RELIES ON THE FULFILMENT OF MY DUTIES!

IF THIS TURNS OUT TO BE A WASTE OF MY TIME...

BA BA BA

BA BA?

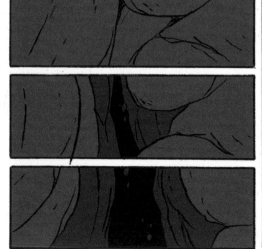

BA

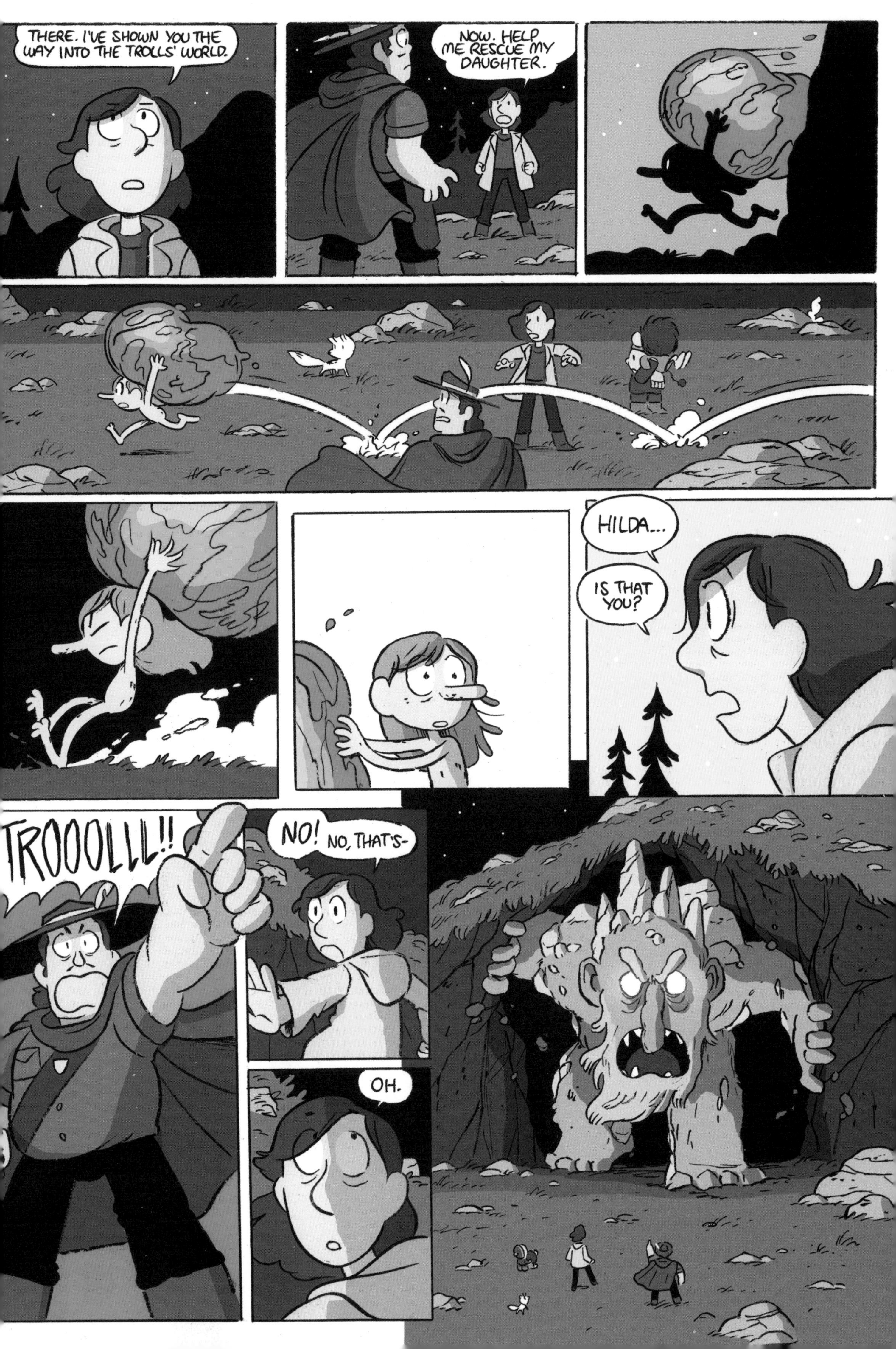

THERE. I'VE SHOWN YOU THE WAY INTO THE TROLLS' WORLD.
NOW. HELP ME RESCUE MY DAUGHTER.
HILDA...
IS THAT YOU?
TROOOLLL!!
NO!
NO, THAT'S-
OH.

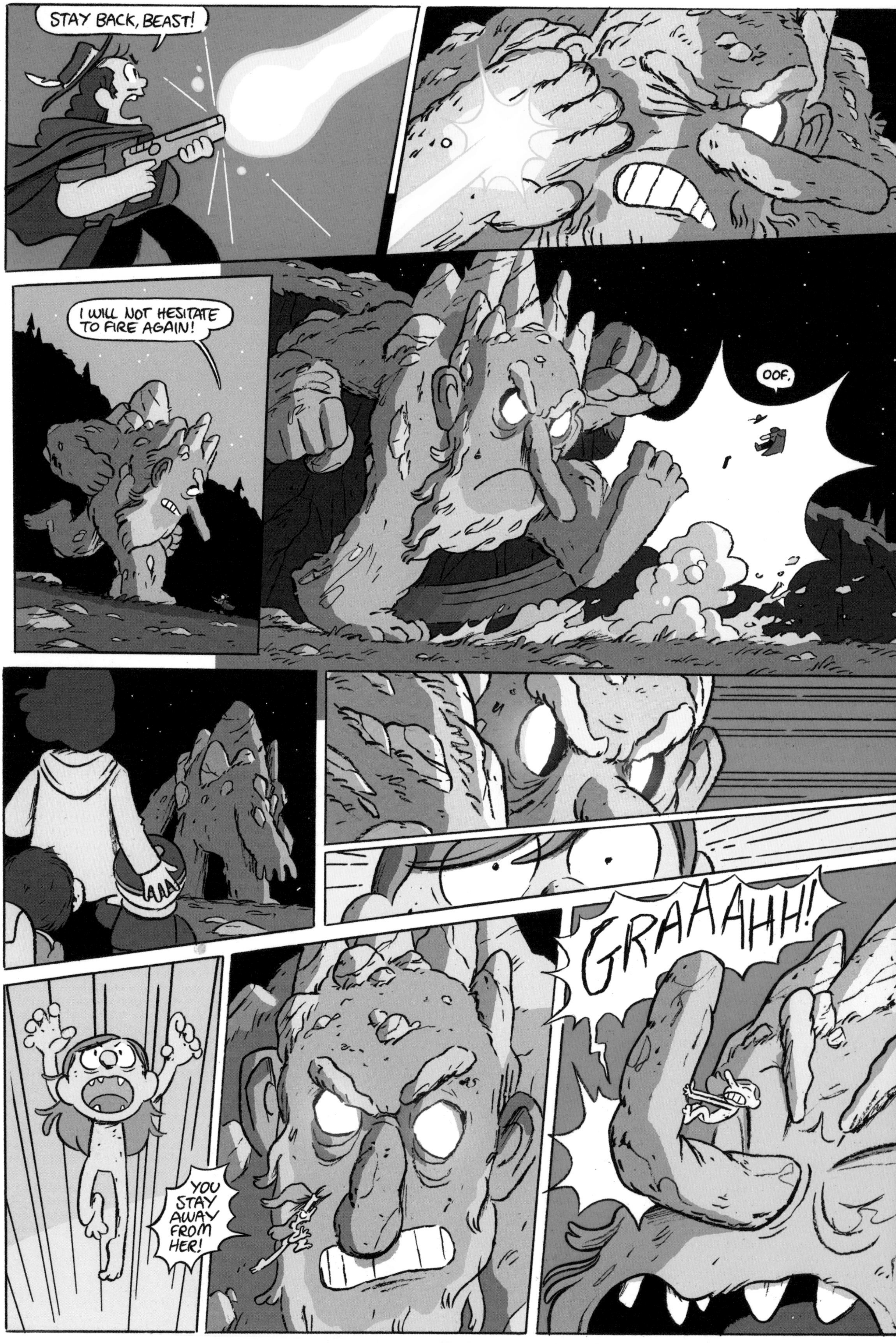
STAY BACK, BEAST!
I WILL NOT HESITATE TO FIRE AGAIN!
OOF.
GRAAAHH!
YOU STAY AWAY FROM HER!

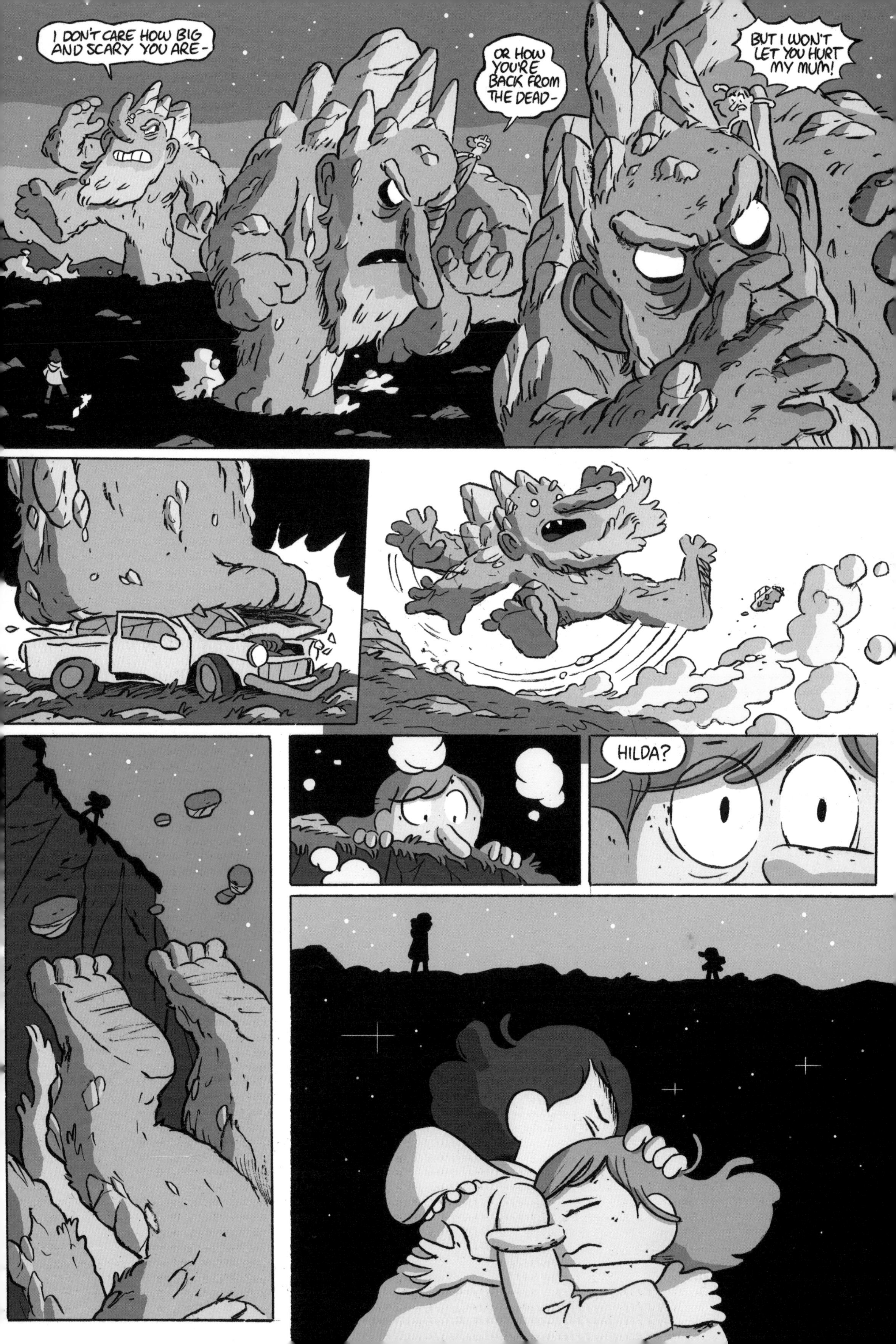
I DON'T CARE HOW BIG AND SCARY YOU ARE-
OR HOW YOU'RE BACK FROM THE DEAD-
BUT I WON'T LET YOU HURT MY MUM!
HILDA?

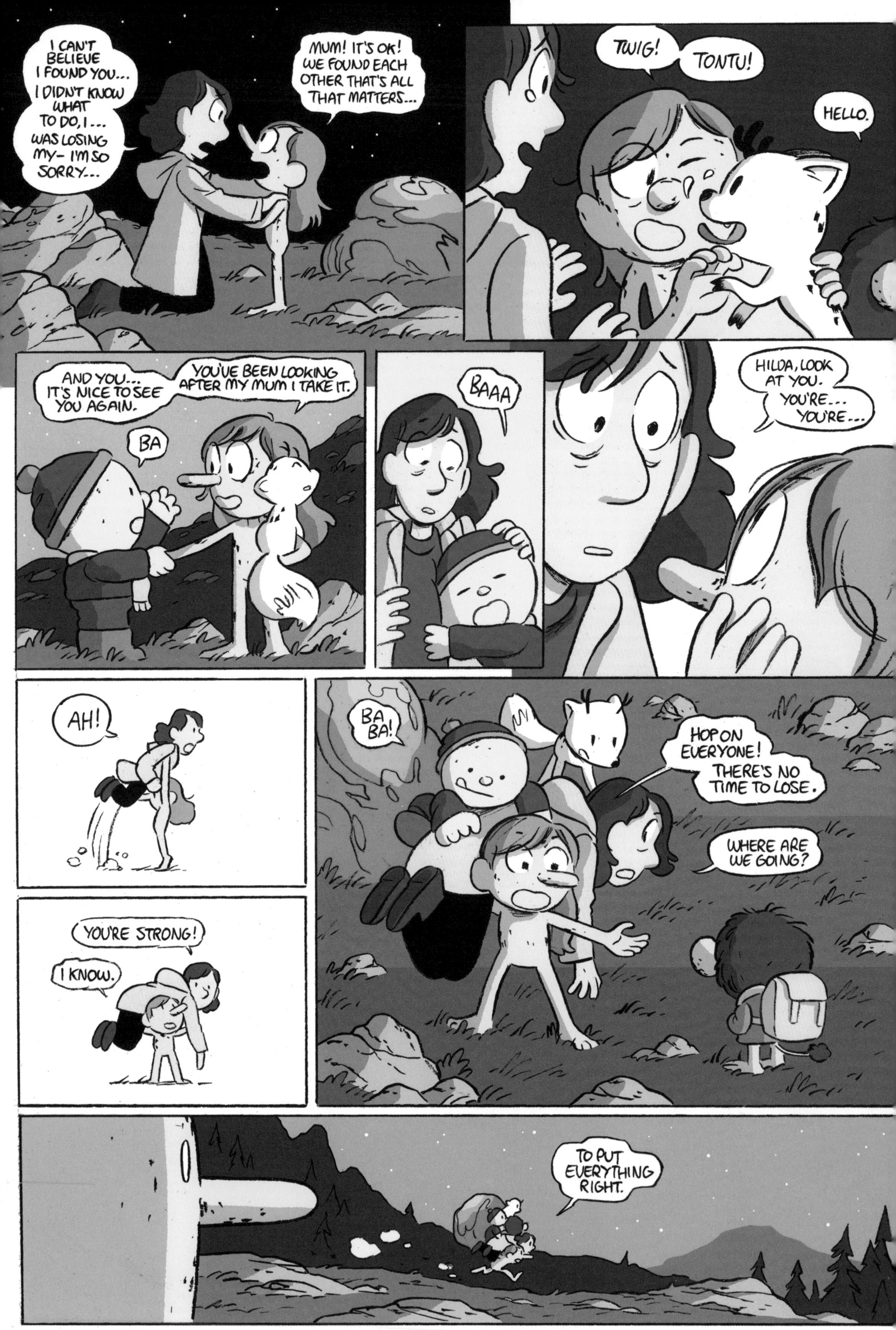

I CAN'T BELIEVE I FOUND YOU... I DIDN'T KNOW WHAT TO DO, I... WAS LOSING MY- I'M SO SORRY...
MUM! IT'S OK! WE FOUND EACH OTHER THAT'S ALL THAT MATTERS...
TWIG!
TONTU!
HELLO.
AND YOU... IT'S NICE TO SEE YOU AGAIN.
YOU'VE BEEN LOOKING AFTER MY MUM I TAKE IT.
BA
BAAA
HILDA, LOOK AT YOU. YOU'RE... YOU'RE...
AH!
YOU'RE STRONG!
I KNOW.
BA BA!
HOP ON EVERYONE! THERE'S NO TIME TO LOSE.
WHERE ARE WE GOING?
TO PUT EVERYTHING RIGHT.

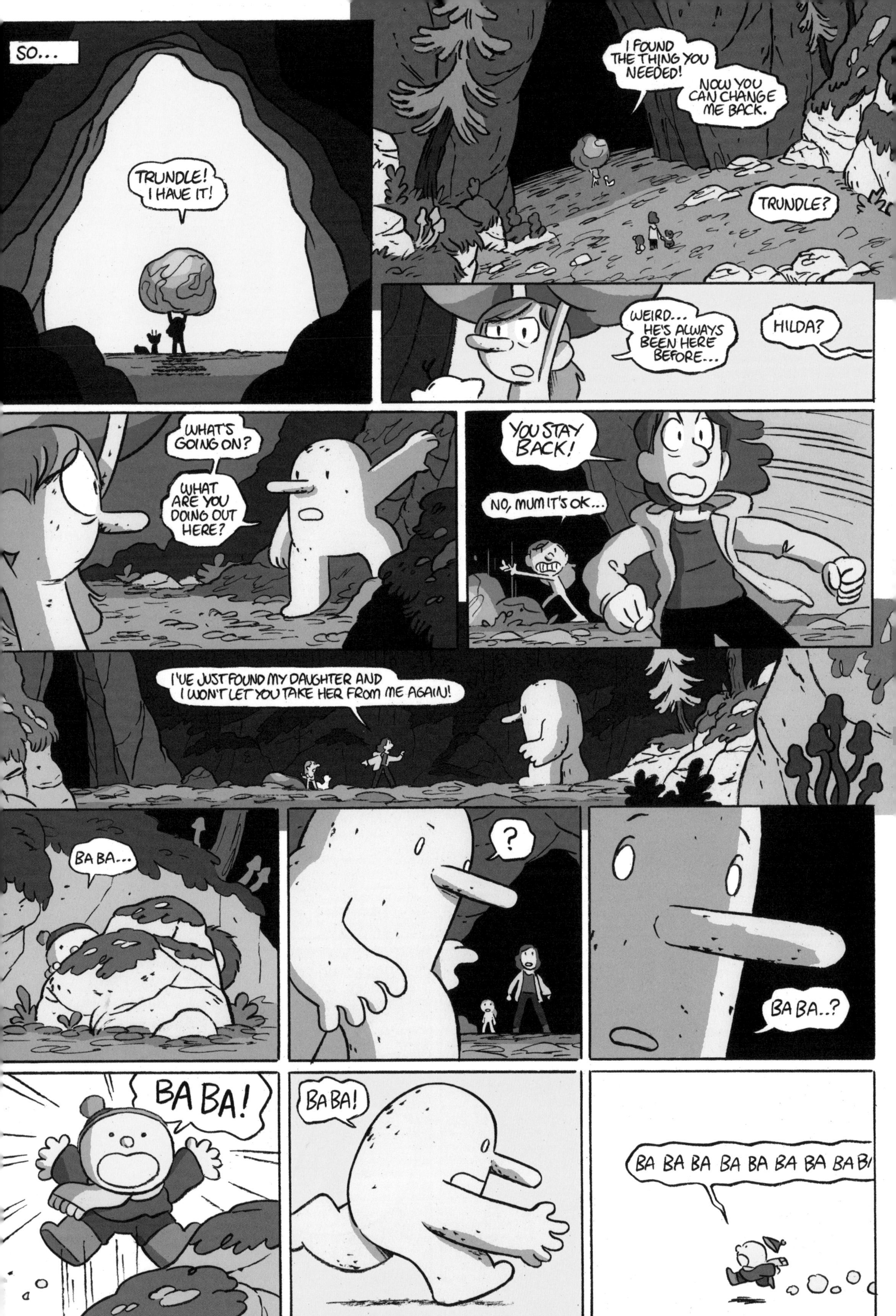
SO...
TRUNDLE! I HAVE IT!
I FOUND THE THING YOU NEEDED!
NOW YOU CAN CHANGE ME BACK.
TRUNDLE?
WEIRD... HE'S ALWAYS BEEN HERE BEFORE...
HILDA?
WHAT'S GOING ON?
WHAT ARE YOU DOING OUT HERE?
YOU STAY BACK!
NO, MUM IT'S OK...
I'VE JUST FOUND MY DAUGHTER AND I WON'T LET YOU TAKE HER FROM ME AGAIN!
BA BA...
?
BA BA..?
BA BA!
BA BA!
BA BA BA BA BA BA BA BA BA

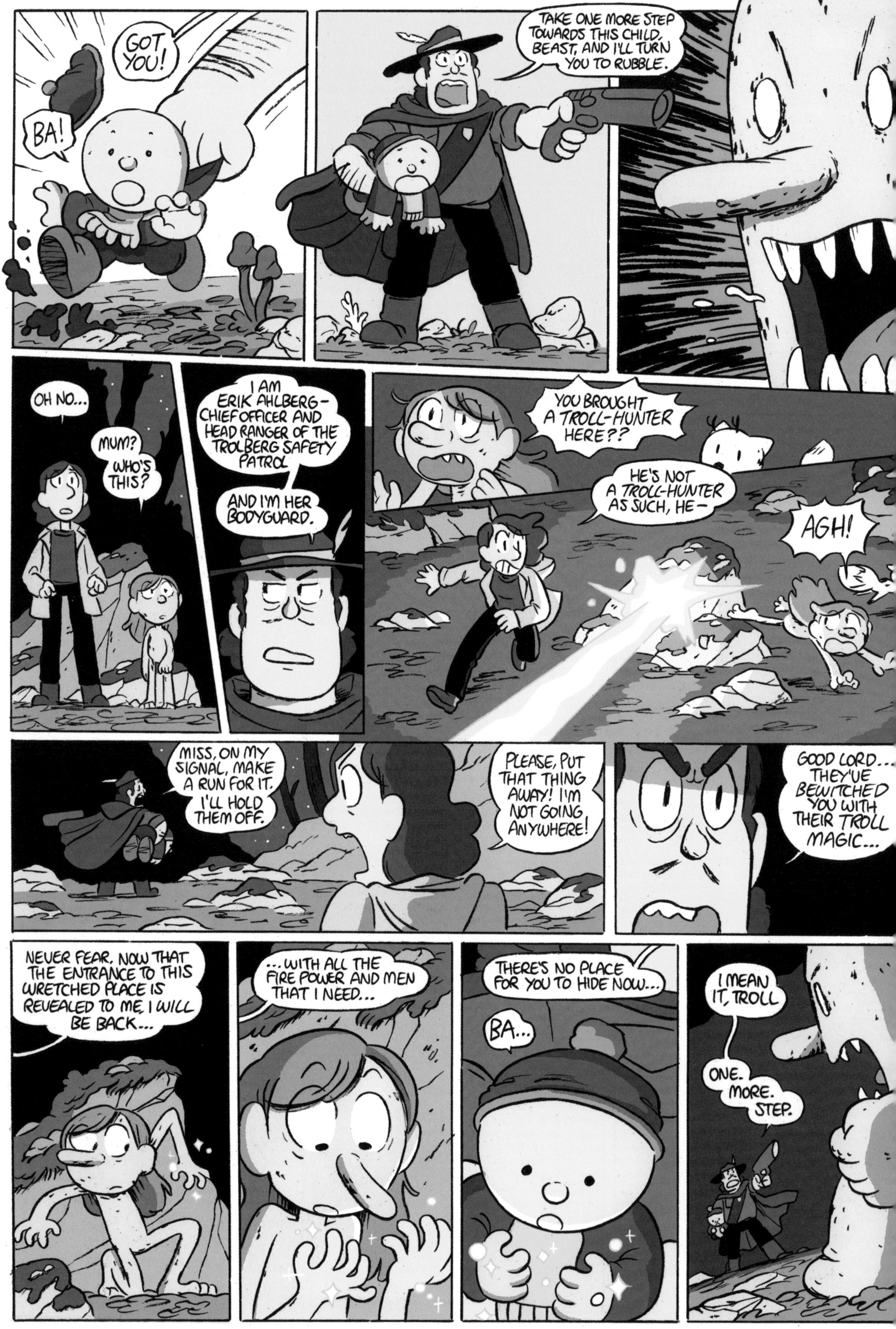
GOT YOU!
BA!
TAKE ONE MORE STEP TOWARDS THIS CHILD, BEAST, AND I'LL TURN YOU TO RUBBLE.
OH NO...
MUM? WHO'S THIS?
I AM ERIK AHLBERG- CHIEF OFFICER AND HEAD RANGER OF THE TROLBERG SAFETY PATROL
AND I'M HER BODYGUARD.
YOU BROUGHT A TROLL-HUNTER HERE??
HE'S NOT A TROLL-HUNTER AS SUCH, HE-
AGH!
MISS, ON MY SIGNAL, MAKE A RUN FOR IT. I'LL HOLD THEM OFF.
PLEASE, PUT THAT THING AWAY! I'M NOT GOING ANYWHERE!
GOOD LORD... THEY'VE BEWITCHED YOU WITH THEIR TROLL MAGIC...
NEVER FEAR. NOW THAT THE ENTRANCE TO THIS WRETCHED PLACE IS REVEALED TO ME, I WILL BE BACK...
...WITH ALL THE FIRE POWER AND MEN THAT I NEED...
THERE'S NO PLACE FOR YOU TO HIDE NOW...
BA...
I MEAN IT, TROLL
ONE. MORE. STEP.

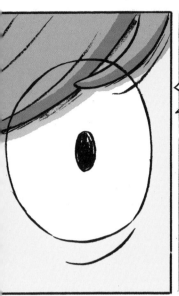

CHOMP

AAAGHAGH!

I'LL TAKE THAT.

MUM!

DON'T WORRY, IT'S JUST A TORCH.

NO IT'S NOT THAT...

IT'S JUST THAT... UM... HI...

HILDA YOU'RE... YOU'RE...

YEP, I'M DEFINITELY BACK AND I, UH...

I DON'T HAVE ANY CLOTHES.

OH! WELL I SUPPOSE BABA WON'T NEED HERS ANYMORE SO...

BA BA BA BA BA BA!

OH...

THANK GOODNESS TONTU CAME ALONG. I BROUGHT SPARES.

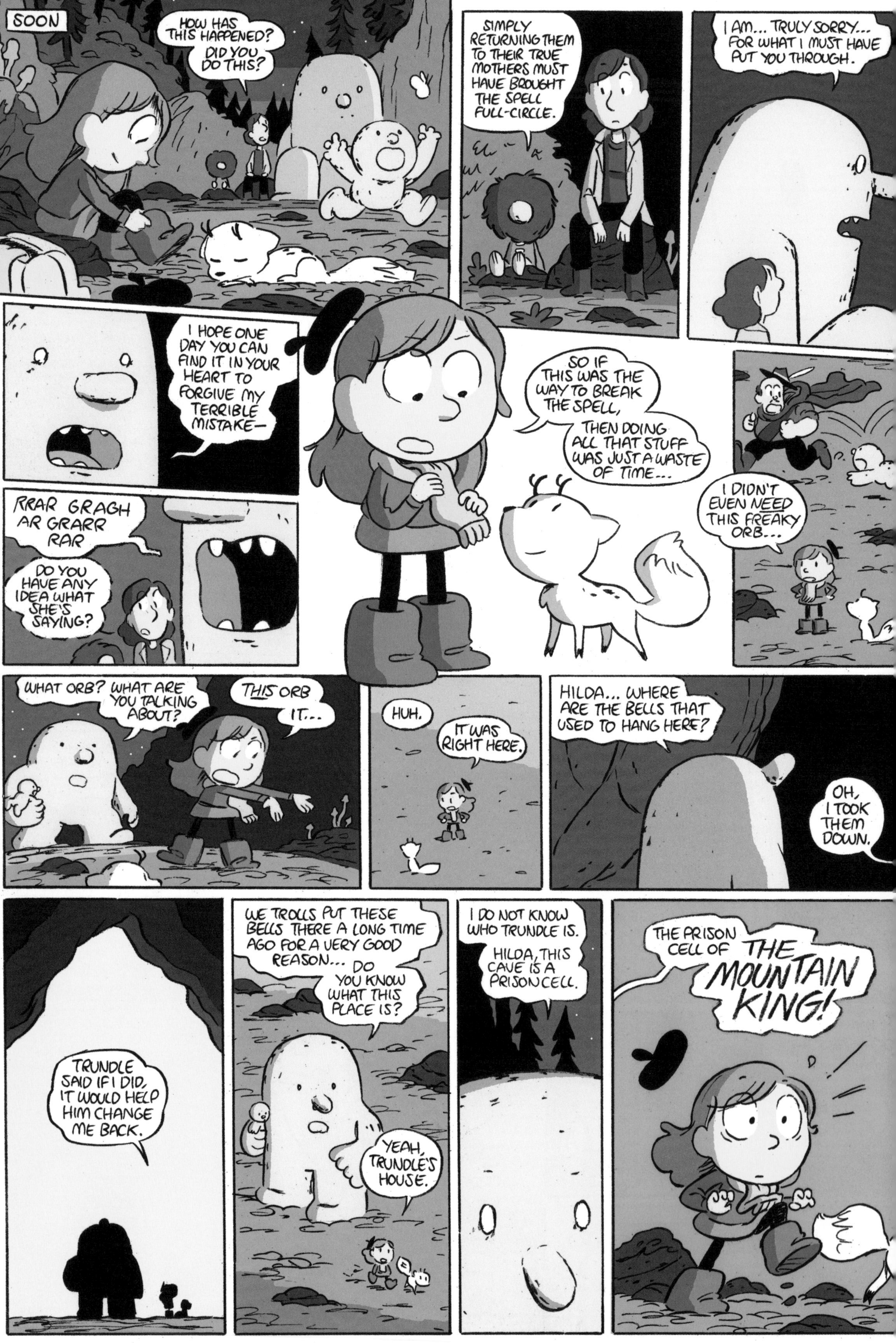
SOON
HOW HAS THIS HAPPENED? DID YOU DO THIS?
SIMPLY RETURNING THEM TO THEIR TRUE MOTHERS MUST HAVE BROUGHT THE SPELL FULL-CIRCLE.
I AM... TRULY SORRY... FOR WHAT I MUST HAVE PUT YOU THROUGH.
I HOPE ONE DAY YOU CAN FIND IT IN YOUR HEART TO FORGIVE MY TERRIBLE MISTAKE—
RRAR GRAGH AR GRARR RAR
DO YOU HAVE ANY IDEA WHAT SHE'S SAYING?
SO IF THIS WAS THE WAY TO BREAK THE SPELL,
THEN DOING ALL THAT STUFF WAS JUST A WASTE OF TIME...
I DIDN'T EVEN NEED THIS FREAKY ORB...
WHAT ORB? WHAT ARE YOU TALKING ABOUT?
THIS ORB
IT...
HUH.
IT WAS RIGHT HERE.
HILDA... WHERE ARE THE BELLS THAT USED TO HANG HERE?
OH, I TOOK THEM DOWN.
TRUNDLE SAID IF I DID, IT WOULD HELP HIM CHANGE ME BACK.
WE TROLLS PUT THESE BELLS THERE A LONG TIME AGO FOR A VERY GOOD REASON... DO YOU KNOW WHAT THIS PLACE IS?
YEAH, TRUNDLE'S HOUSE.
I DO NOT KNOW WHO TRUNDLE IS.
HILDA, THIS CAVE IS A PRISON CELL.
THE PRISON CELL OF THE MOUNTAIN KING!

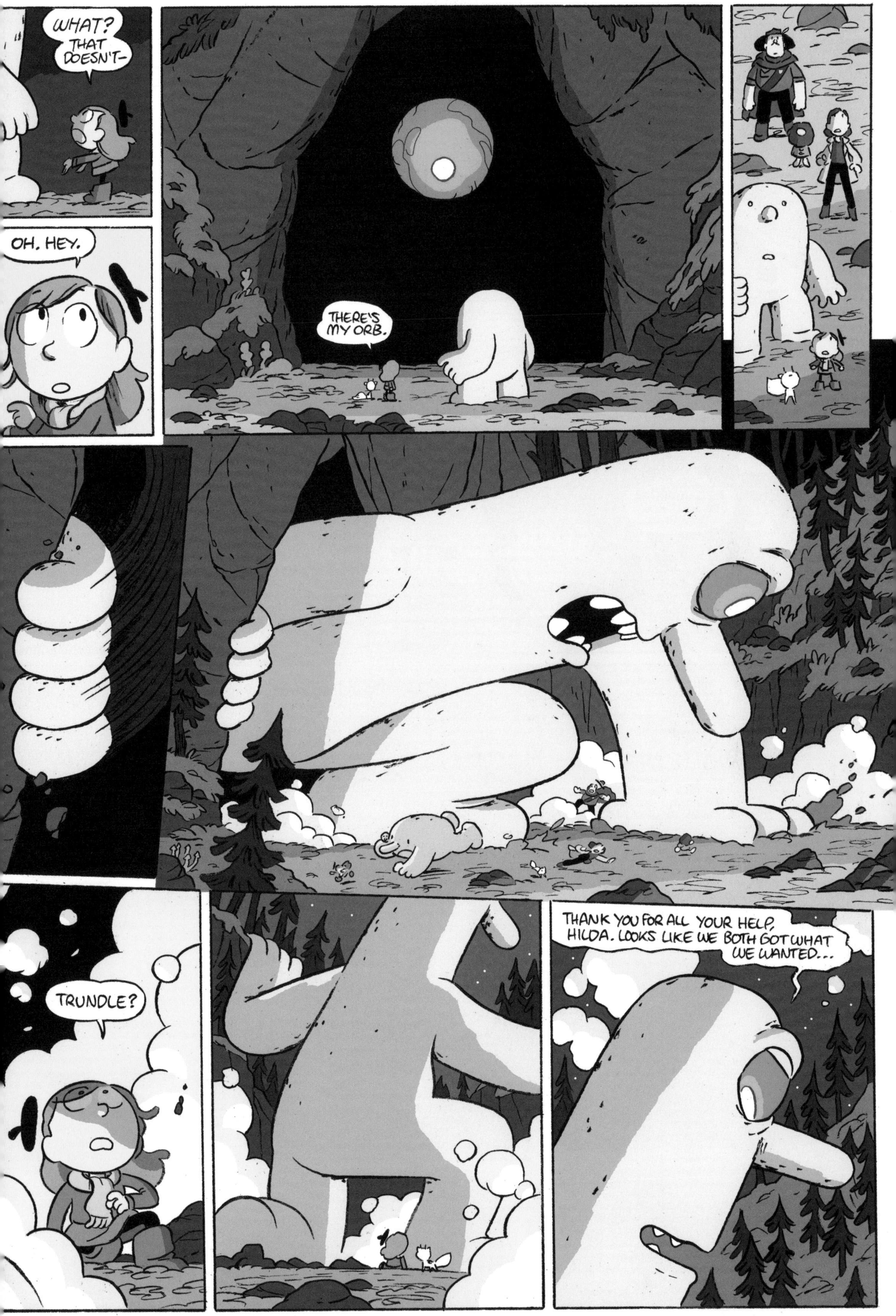
WHAT? THAT DOESN'T-
OH. HEY.
THERE'S MY ORB.
TRUNDLE?
THANK YOU FOR ALL YOUR HELP, HILDA. LOOKS LIKE WE BOTH GOT WHAT WE WANTED...

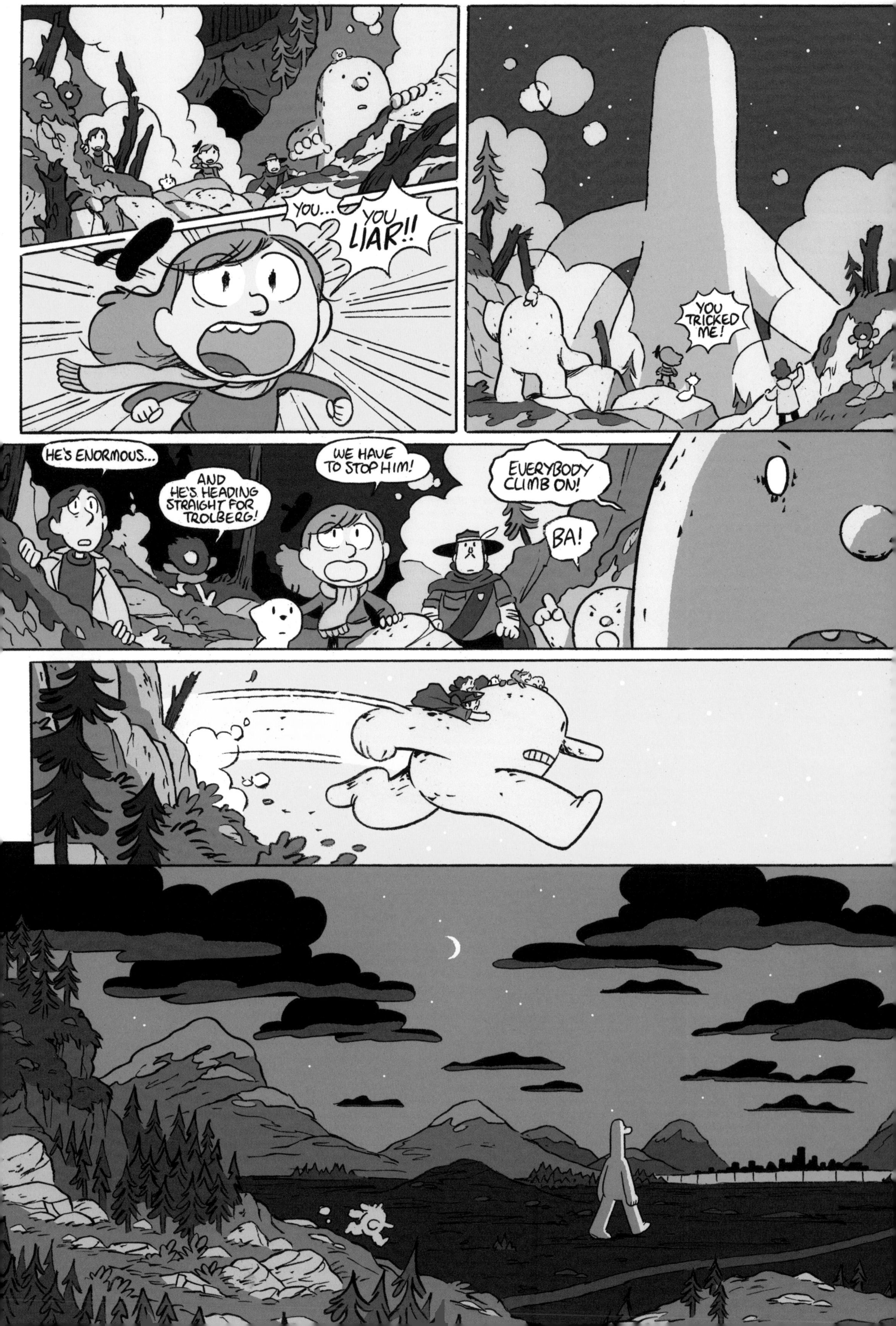
YOU...
YOU LIAR!!
YOU TRICKED ME!
HE'S ENORMOUS...
AND HE'S HEADING STRAIGHT FOR TROLBERG!
WE HAVE TO STOP HIM!
EVERYBODY CLIMB ON!
BA!

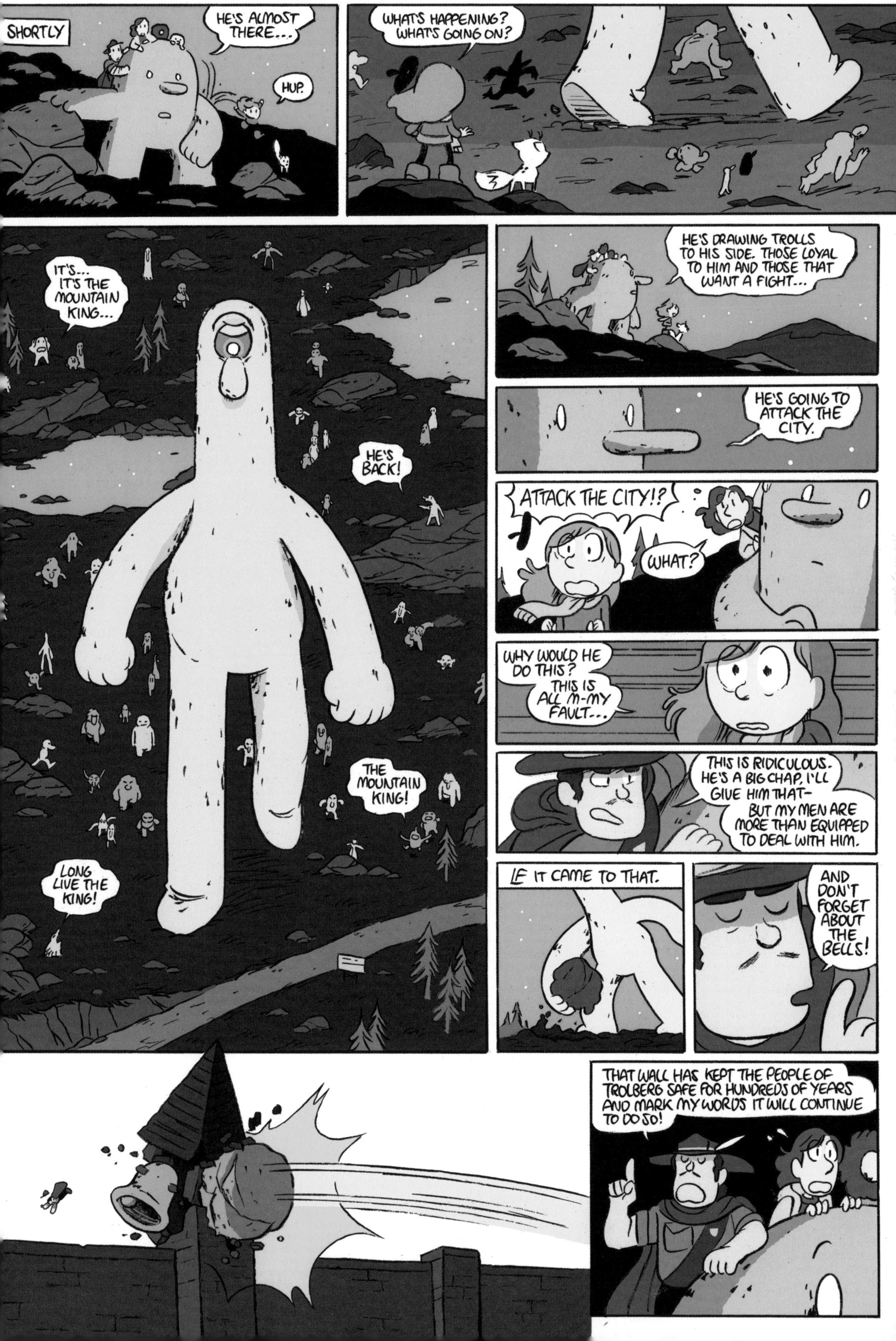

SHORTLY
HE'S ALMOST THERE...
HUP.
WHAT'S HAPPENING? WHAT'S GOING ON?
IT'S... IT'S THE MOUNTAIN KING...
HE'S BACK!
THE MOUNTAIN KING!
LONG LIVE THE KING!
HE'S DRAWING TROLLS TO HIS SIDE. THOSE LOYAL TO HIM AND THOSE THAT WANT A FIGHT...
HE'S GOING TO ATTACK THE CITY.
ATTACK THE CITY!?
WHAT?
WHY WOULD HE DO THIS?
THIS IS ALL M-MY FAULT...
THIS IS RIDICULOUS. HE'S A BIG CHAP, I'LL GIVE HIM THAT-
BUT MY MEN ARE MORE THAN EQUIPPED TO DEAL WITH HIM.
IF IT CAME TO THAT.
AND DON'T FORGET ABOUT THE BELLS!
THAT WALL HAS KEPT THE PEOPLE OF TROLBERG SAFE FOR HUNDREDS OF YEARS AND MARK MY WORDS IT WILL CONTINUE TO DO SO!

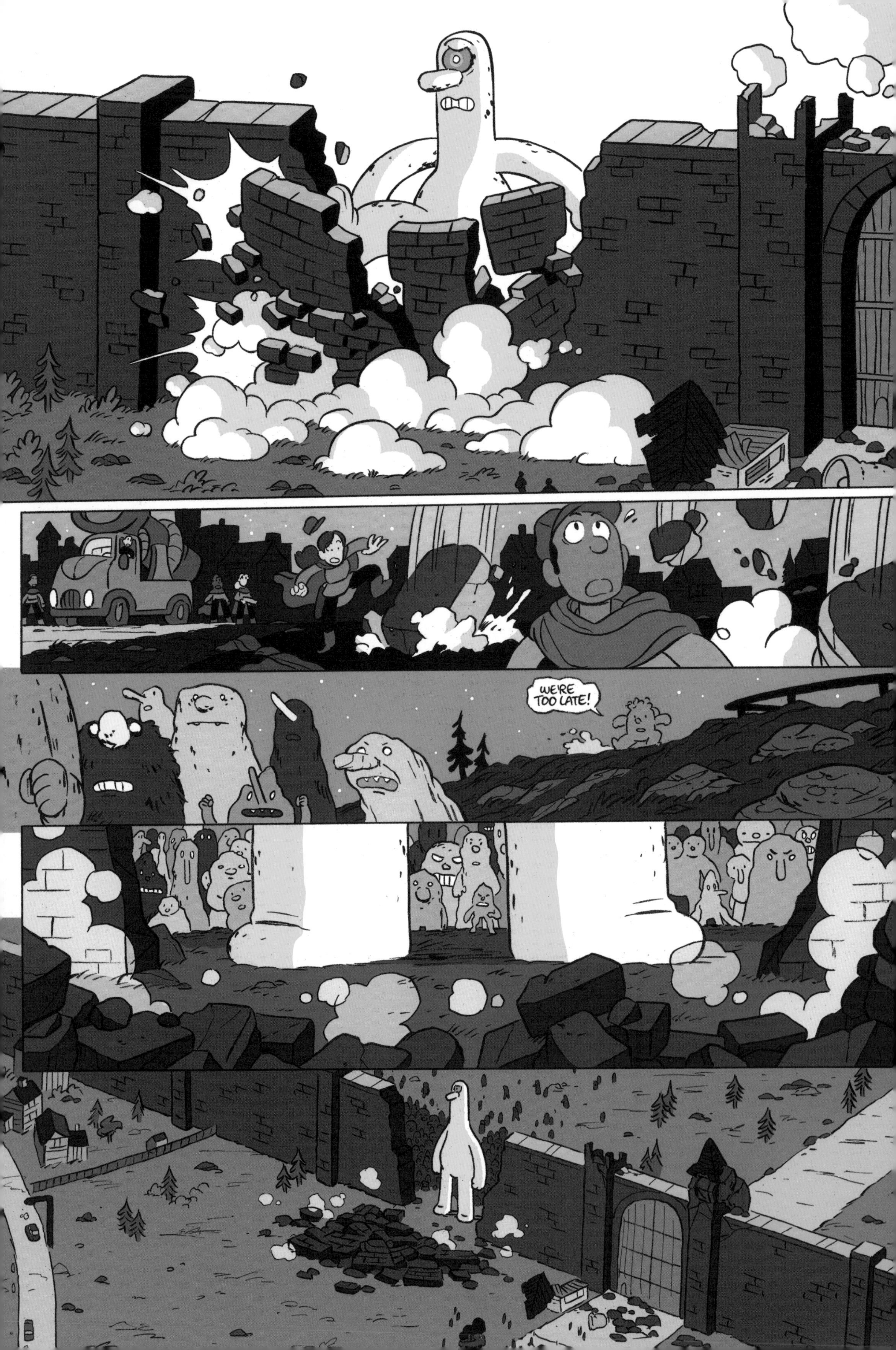
WE'RE TOO LATE!

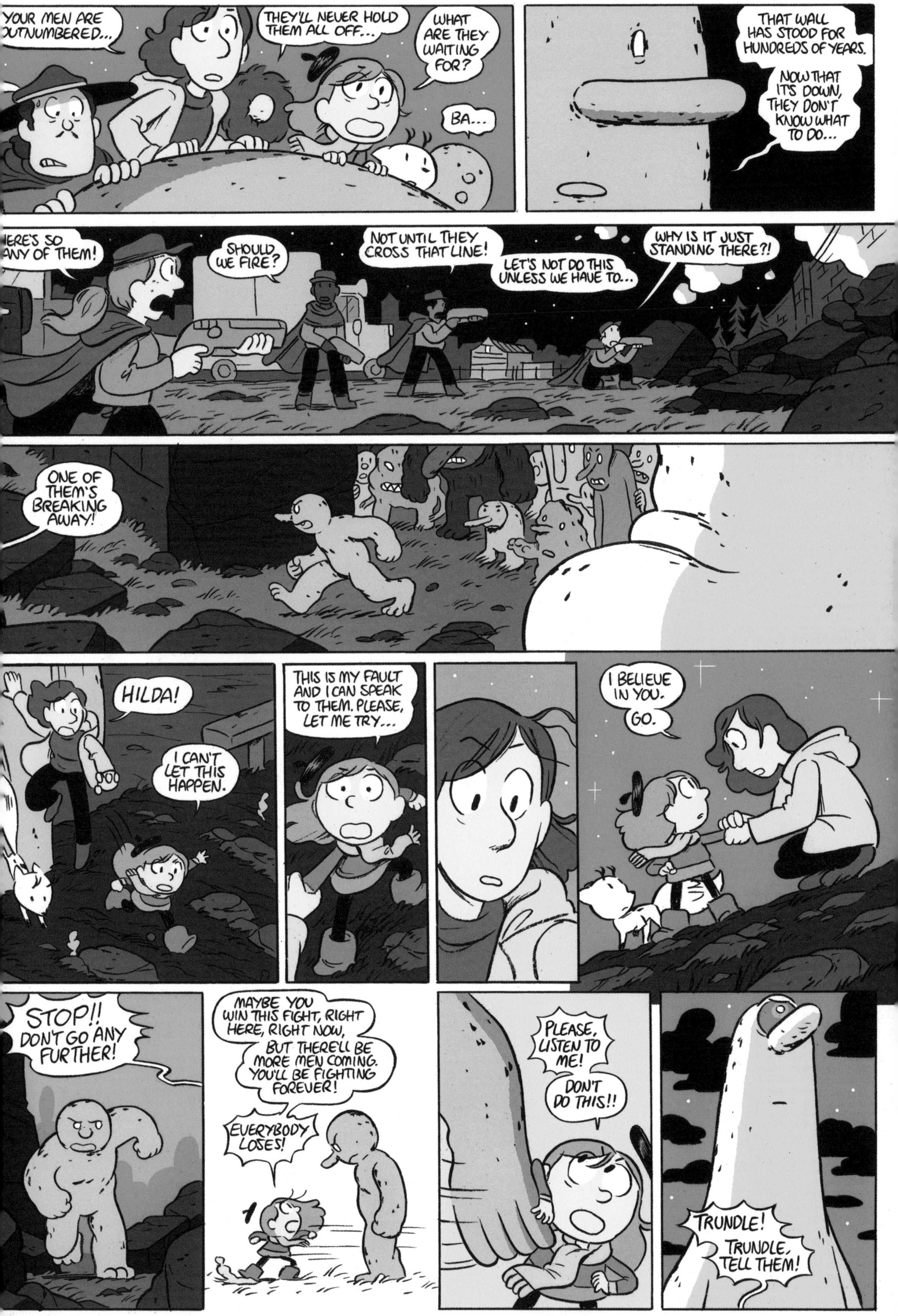

YOUR MEN ARE OUTNUMBERED...
THEY'LL NEVER HOLD THEM ALL OFF...
WHAT ARE THEY WAITING FOR?
BA...
THAT WALL HAS STOOD FOR HUNDREDS OF YEARS.
NOW THAT IT'S DOWN, THEY DON'T KNOW WHAT TO DO...
HERE'S SO ANY OF THEM!
SHOULD WE FIRE?
NOT UNTIL THEY CROSS THAT LINE!
LET'S NOT DO THIS UNLESS WE HAVE TO...
WHY IS IT JUST STANDING THERE?!
ONE OF THEM'S BREAKING AWAY!
HILDA!
I CAN'T LET THIS HAPPEN.
THIS IS MY FAULT AND I CAN SPEAK TO THEM. PLEASE, LET ME TRY...
I BELIEVE IN YOU.
GO.
STOP!! DON'T GO ANY FURTHER!
MAYBE YOU WIN THIS FIGHT, RIGHT HERE, RIGHT NOW,
BUT THERE'LL BE MORE MEN COMING. YOU'LL BE FIGHTING FOREVER!
EVERYBODY LOSES!
PLEASE, LISTEN TO ME!
DON'T DO THIS!!
TRUNDLE!
TRUNDLE, TELL THEM!

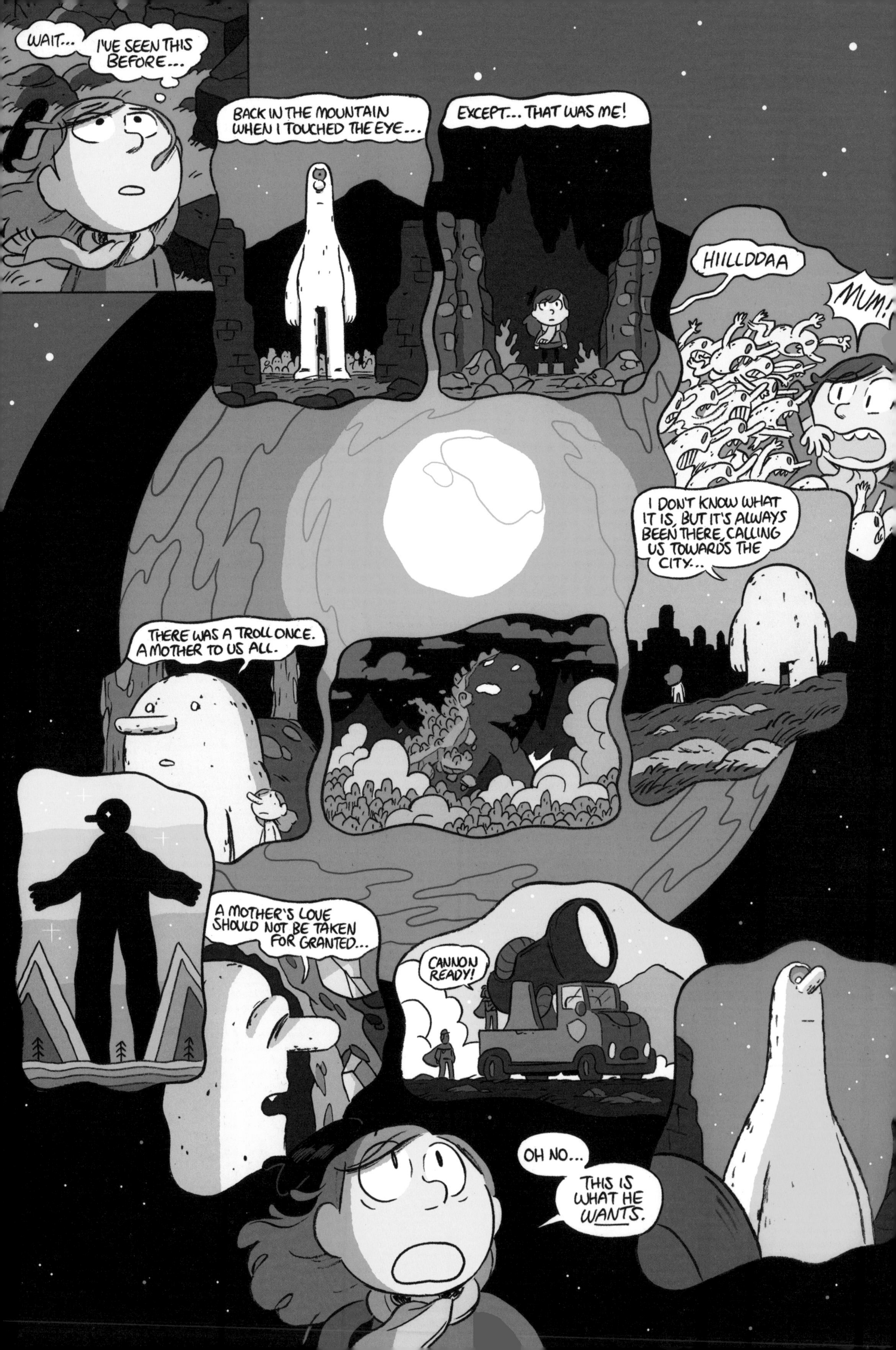
WAIT...
I'VE SEEN THIS BEFORE...
BACK IN THE MOUNTAIN WHEN I TOUCHED THE EYE...
EXCEPT... THAT WAS ME!
HIILLDDAA
MUM!
I DON'T KNOW WHAT IT IS, BUT IT'S ALWAYS BEEN THERE, CALLING US TOWARDS THE CITY...
THERE WAS A TROLL ONCE. A MOTHER TO US ALL.
A MOTHER'S LOVE SHOULD NOT BE TAKEN FOR GRANTED...
CANNON READY!
OH NO...
THIS IS WHAT HE WANTS.

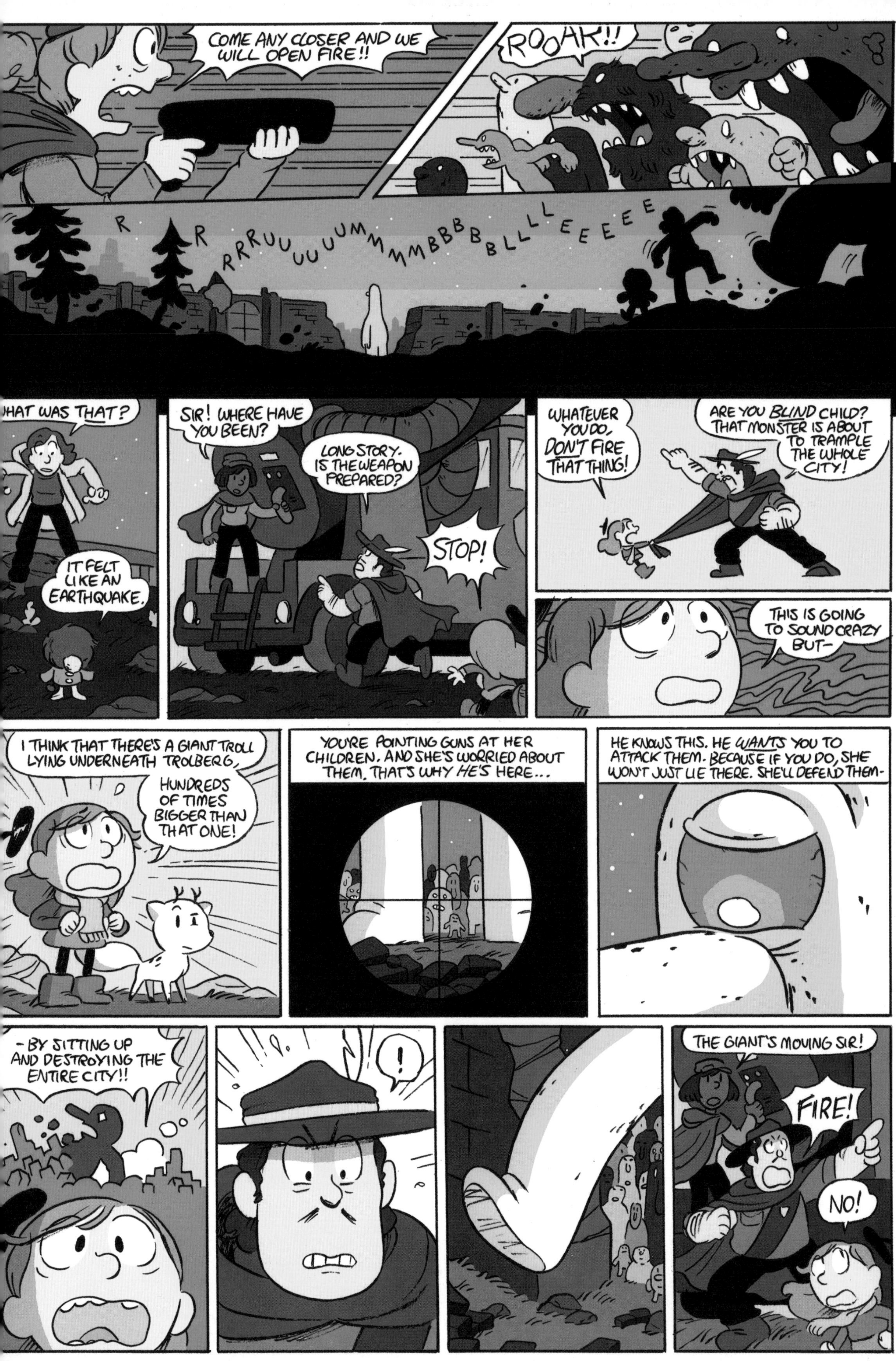

COME ANY CLOSER AND WE WILL OPEN FIRE!!
ROOAR!!
R R RRRUUUUUMMMMMBBBBBLLLLEEEEEE
WHAT WAS THAT?
IT FELT LIKE AN EARTHQUAKE.
SIR! WHERE HAVE YOU BEEN?
LONG STORY. IS THE WEAPON PREPARED?
STOP!
WHATEVER YOU DO, DON'T FIRE THAT THING!
ARE YOU BLIND CHILD? THAT MONSTER IS ABOUT TO TRAMPLE THE WHOLE CITY!
THIS IS GOING TO SOUND CRAZY BUT-
I THINK THAT THERE'S A GIANT TROLL LYING UNDERNEATH TROLBERG,
HUNDREDS OF TIMES BIGGER THAN THAT ONE!
YOU'RE POINTING GUNS AT HER CHILDREN. AND SHE'S WORRIED ABOUT THEM. THAT'S WHY HE'S HERE...
HE KNOWS THIS. HE WANTS YOU TO ATTACK THEM. BECAUSE IF YOU DO, SHE WON'T JUST LIE THERE. SHE'LL DEFEND THEM-
-BY SITTING UP AND DESTROYING THE ENTIRE CITY!!
!
THE GIANT'S MOVING SIR!
FIRE!
NO!

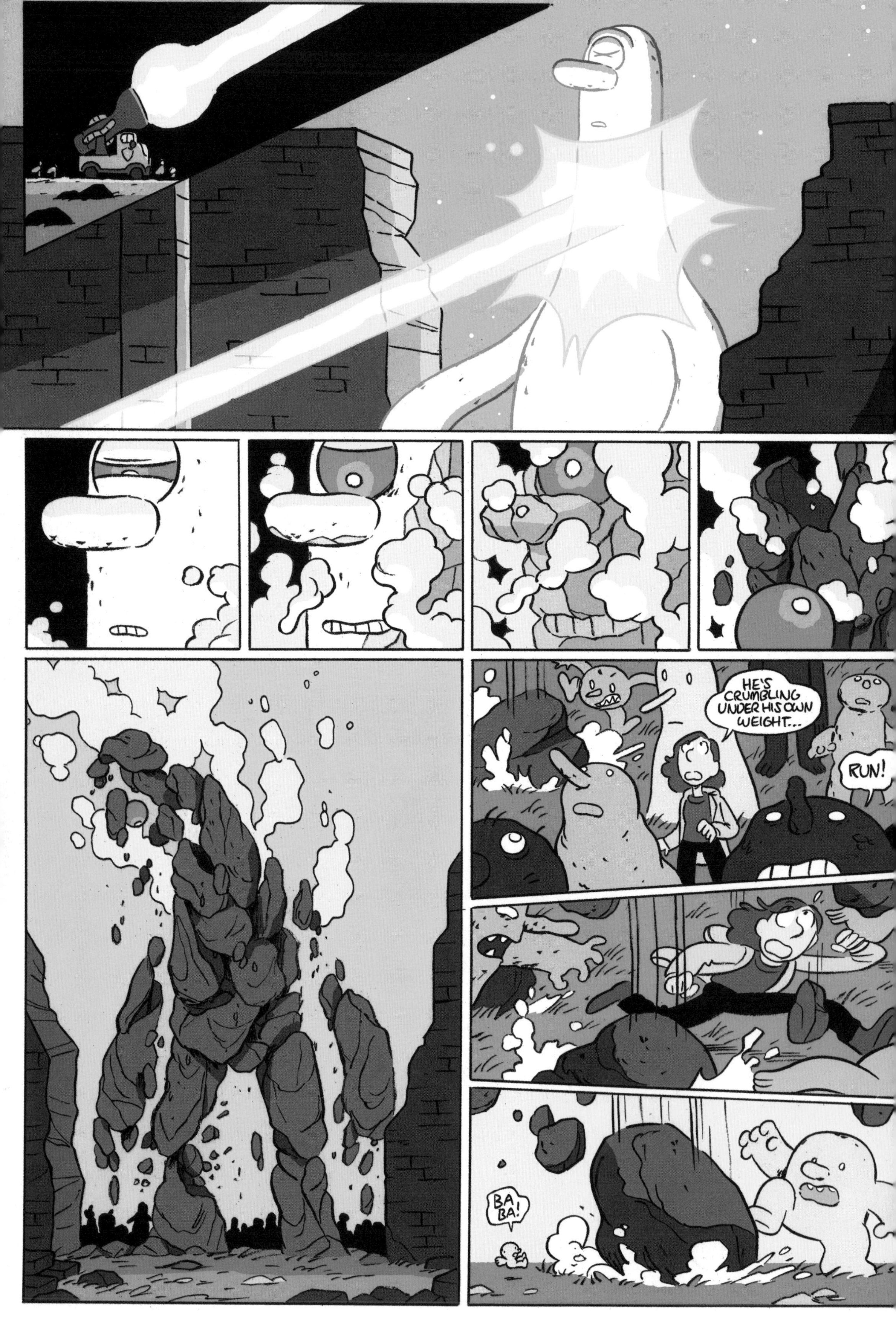
HE'S CRUMBLING UNDER HIS OWN WEIGHT...
RUN!
BA BA!

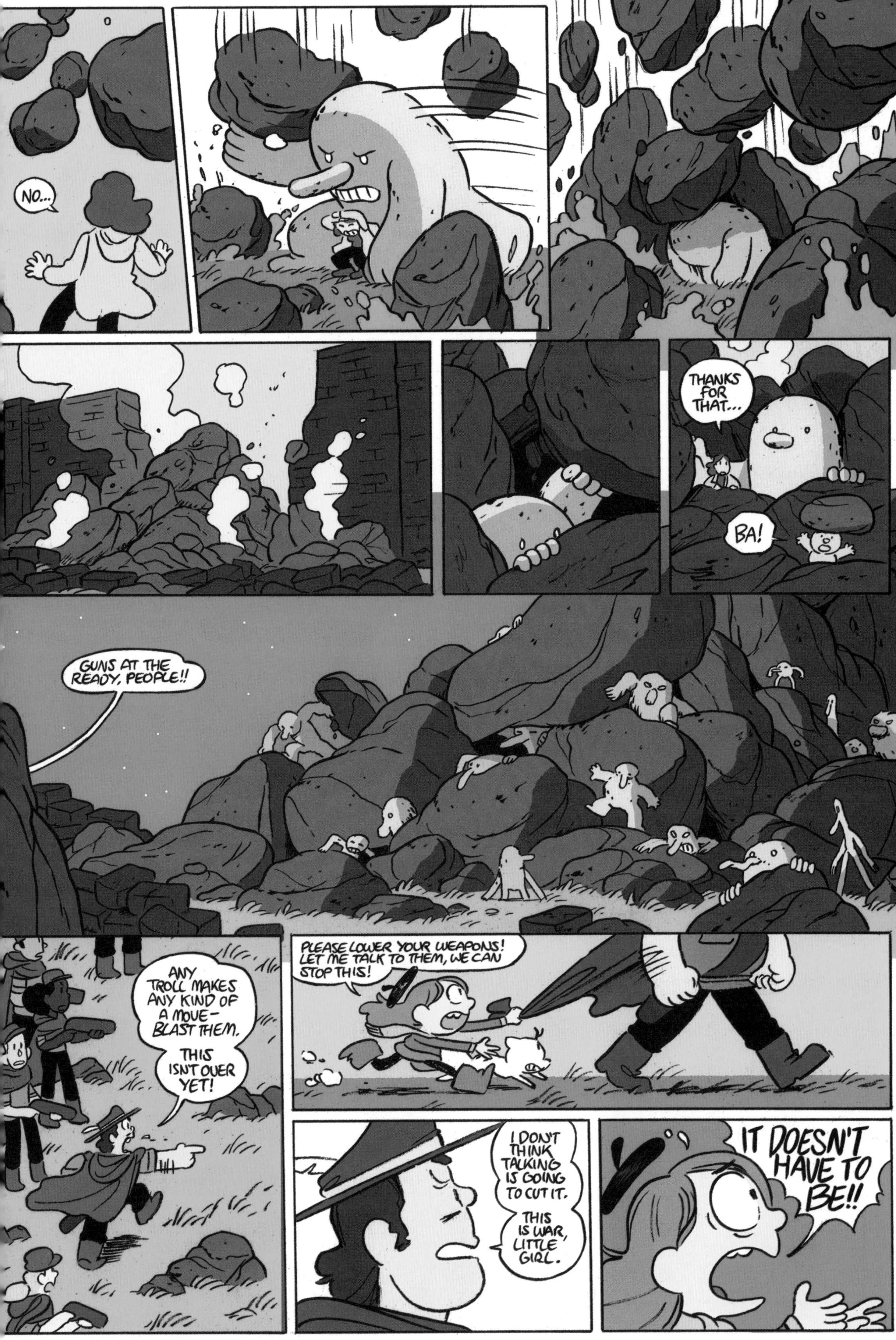
NO...
THANKS FOR THAT...
BA!
GUNS AT THE READY, PEOPLE!!
ANY TROLL MAKES ANY KIND OF A MOVE- BLAST THEM.
THIS ISN'T OVER YET!
PLEASE LOWER YOUR WEAPONS! LET ME TALK TO THEM, WE CAN STOP THIS!
I DON'T THINK TALKING IS GOING TO CUT IT.
THIS IS WAR, LITTLE GIRL.
IT DOESN'T HAVE TO BE!!

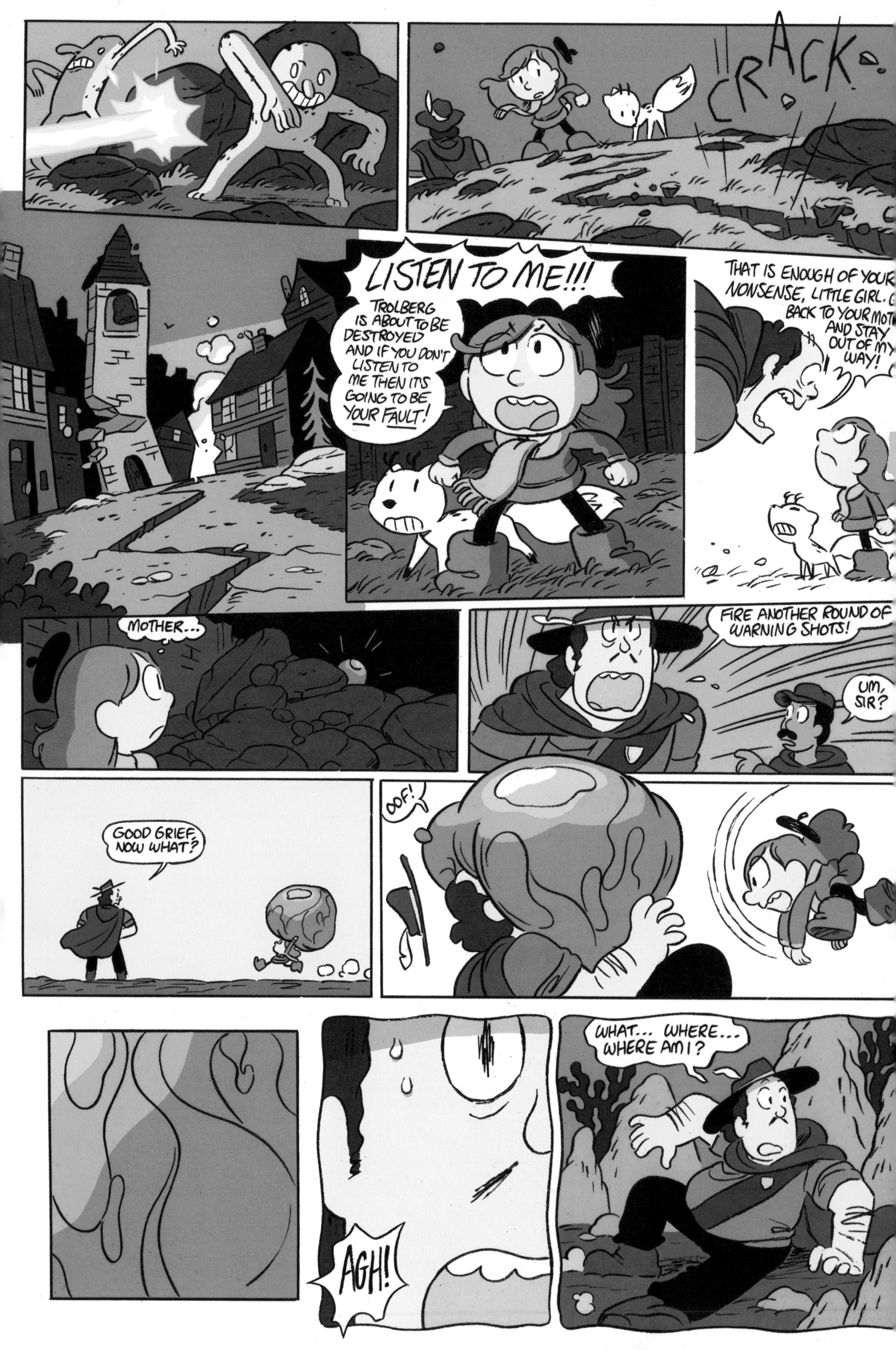
CRACK!
LISTEN TO ME!!!
TROLBERG IS ABOUT TO BE DESTROYED AND IF YOU DON'T LISTEN TO ME THEN IT'S GOING TO BE YOUR FAULT!
THAT IS ENOUGH OF YOUR NONSENSE, LITTLE GIRL.
AND STAY OUT OF MY WAY!
MOTHER...
FIRE ANOTHER ROUND OF WARNING SHOTS!
UM, SIR?
GOOD GRIEF, NOW WHAT?
OOF!
AGH!
WHAT... WHERE... WHERE AM I?

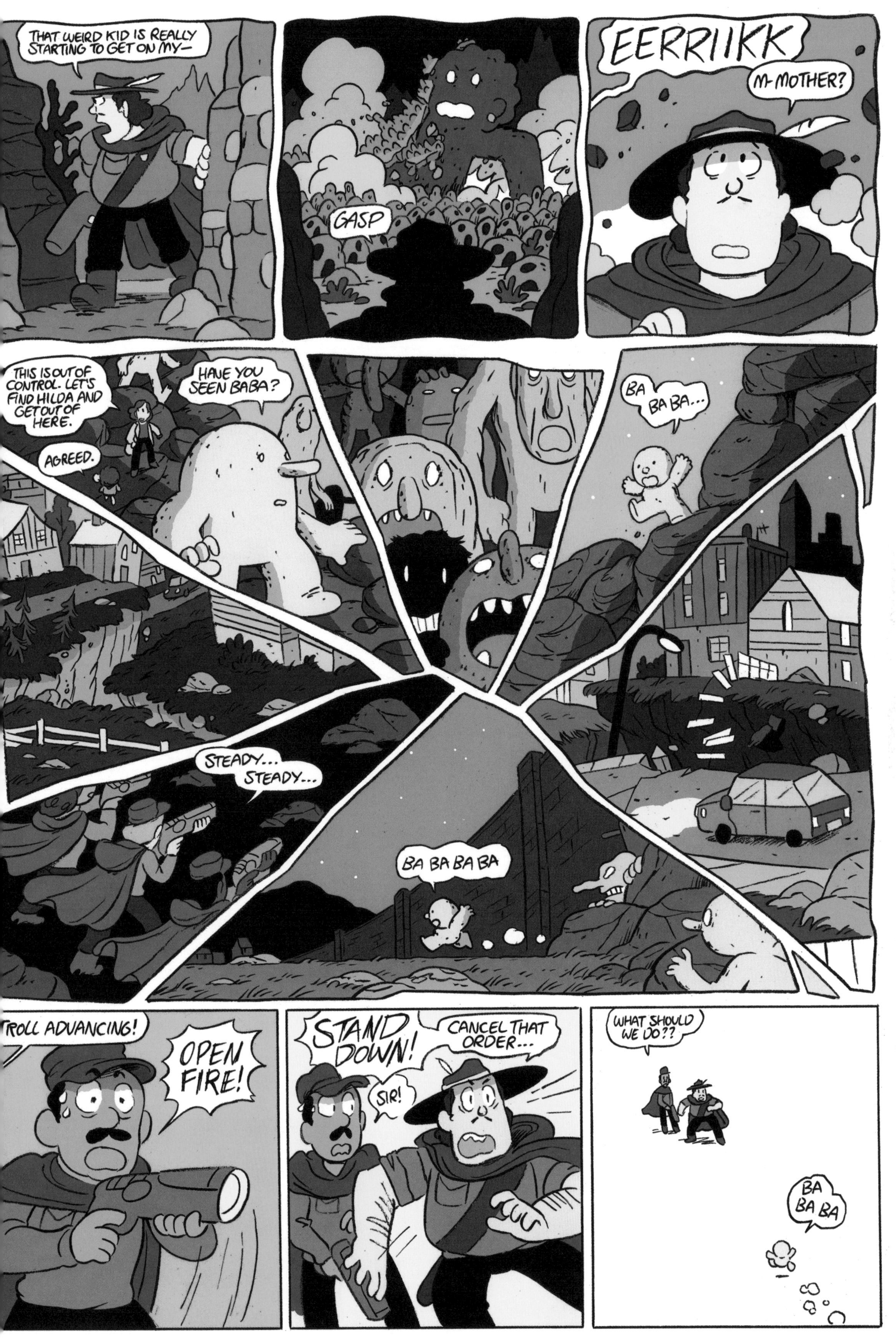
THAT WEIRD KID IS REALLY STARTING TO GET ON MY—
GASP
EERRIIKK
M-MOTHER?
THIS IS OUT OF CONTROL. LET'S FIND HILDA AND GET OUT OF HERE.
AGREED.
HAVE YOU SEEN BABA?
BA BA BA...
STEADY... STEADY...
BA BA BA BA
TROLL ADVANCING!
OPEN FIRE!
STAND DOWN!
SIR!
CANCEL THAT ORDER...
WHAT SHOULD WE DO??
BA BA BA

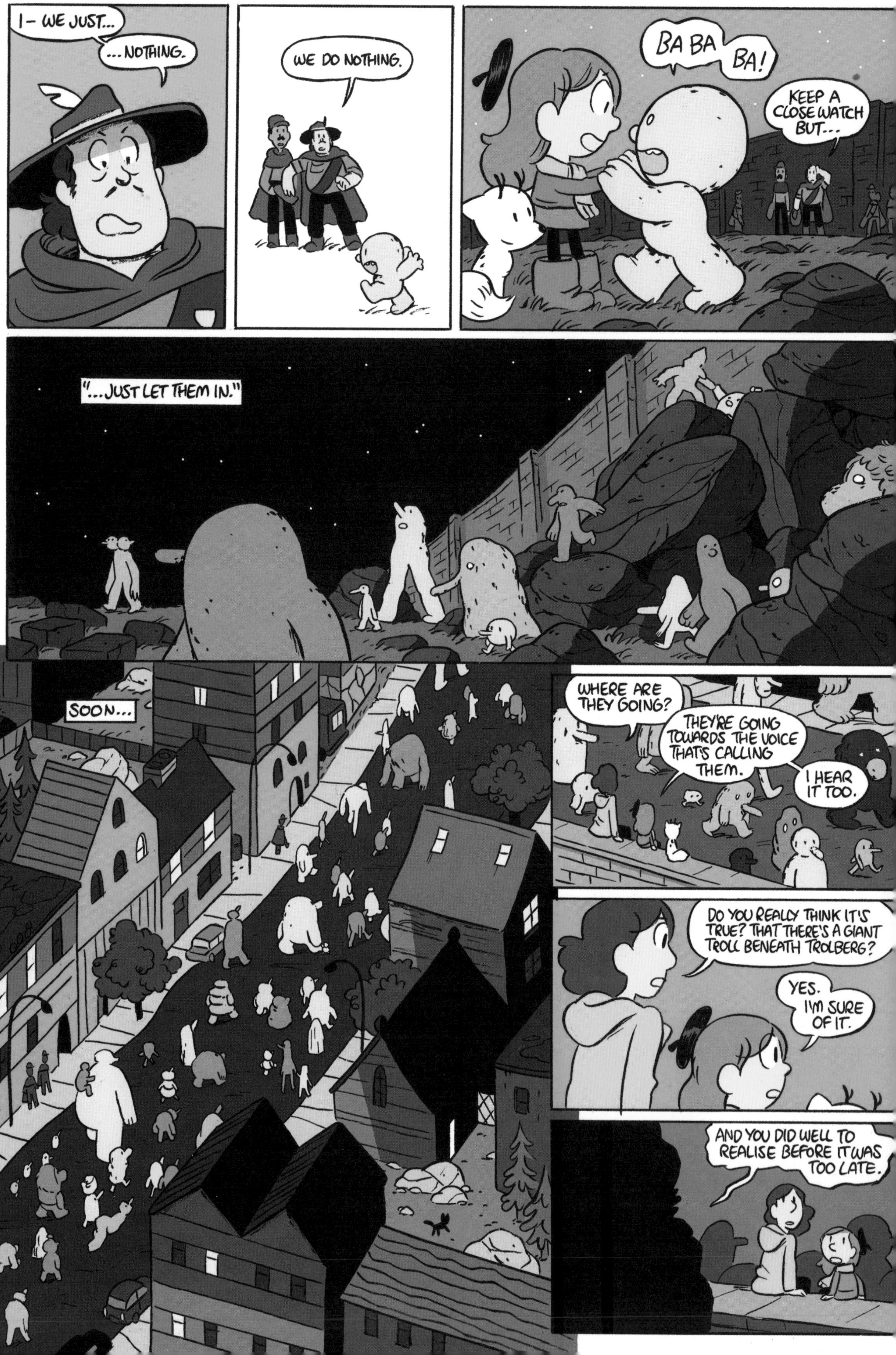
I- WE JUST...
...NOTHING.
WE DO NOTHING.
BA BA BA!
KEEP A CLOSE WATCH BUT...
"...JUST LET THEM IN."
SOON...
WHERE ARE THEY GOING?
THEY'RE GOING TOWARDS THE VOICE THAT'S CALLING THEM.
I HEAR IT TOO.
DO YOU REALLY THINK IT'S TRUE? THAT THERE'S A GIANT TROLL BENEATH TROLBERG?
YES. I'M SURE OF IT.
AND YOU DID WELL TO REALISE BEFORE IT WAS TOO LATE.

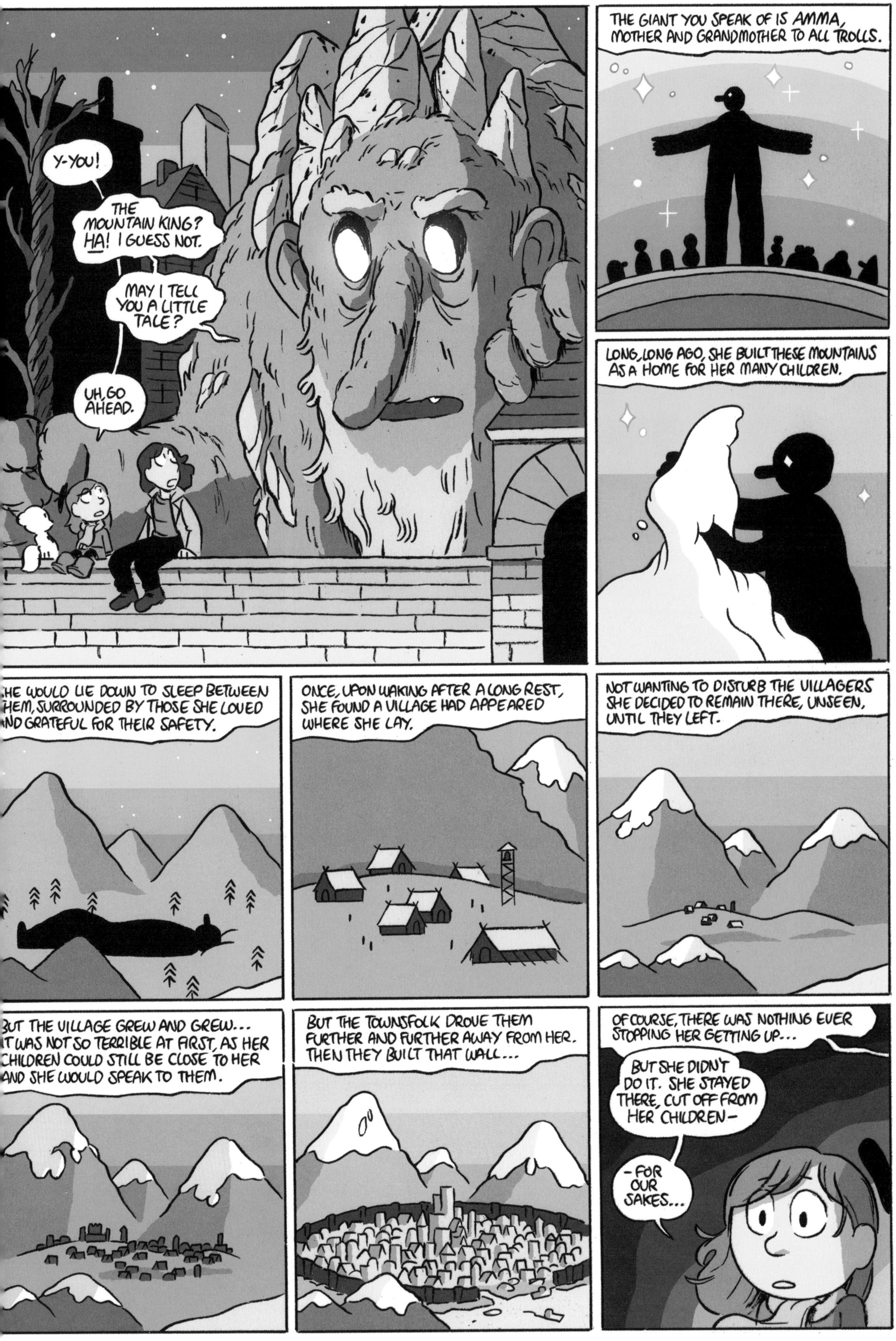

Y-YOU!
THE MOUNTAIN KING? HA! I GUESS NOT.
MAY I TELL YOU A LITTLE TALE?
UH, GO AHEAD.
THE GIANT YOU SPEAK OF IS AMMA, MOTHER AND GRANDMOTHER TO ALL TROLLS.
LONG, LONG AGO, SHE BUILT THESE MOUNTAINS AS A HOME FOR HER MANY CHILDREN.
SHE WOULD LIE DOWN TO SLEEP BETWEEN THEM, SURROUNDED BY THOSE SHE LOVED AND GRATEFUL FOR THEIR SAFETY.
ONCE, UPON WAKING AFTER A LONG REST, SHE FOUND A VILLAGE HAD APPEARED WHERE SHE LAY.
NOT WANTING TO DISTURB THE VILLAGERS SHE DECIDED TO REMAIN THERE, UNSEEN, UNTIL THEY LEFT.
BUT THE VILLAGE GREW AND GREW... IT WAS NOT SO TERRIBLE AT FIRST, AS HER CHILDREN COULD STILL BE CLOSE TO HER AND SHE WOULD SPEAK TO THEM.
BUT THE TOWNSFOLK DROVE THEM FURTHER AND FURTHER AWAY FROM HER. THEN THEY BUILT THAT WALL...
OF COURSE, THERE WAS NOTHING EVER STOPPING HER GETTING UP...
BUT SHE DIDN'T DO IT. SHE STAYED THERE, CUT OFF FROM HER CHILDREN-
-FOR OUR SAKES...

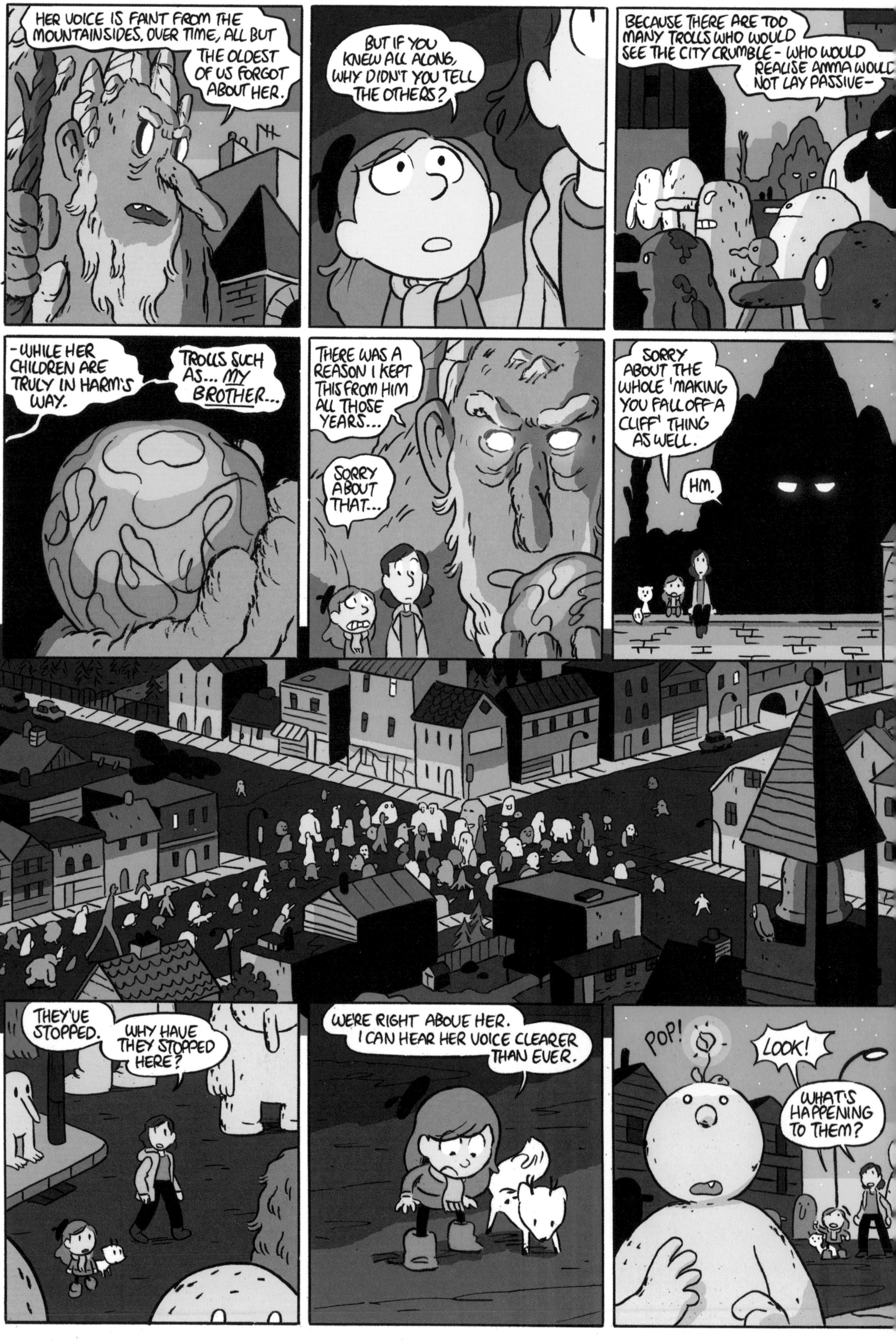
HER VOICE IS FAINT FROM THE MOUNTAINSIDES. OVER TIME, ALL BUT
THE OLDEST OF US FORGOT ABOUT HER.
BUT IF YOU KNEW ALL ALONG, WHY DIDN'T YOU TELL THE OTHERS?
BECAUSE THERE ARE TOO MANY TROLLS WHO WOULD SEE THE CITY CRUMBLE - WHO WOULD
REALISE AMMA WOULD NOT LAY PASSIVE-
-WHILE HER CHILDREN ARE TRULY IN HARM'S WAY.
TROLLS SUCH AS... MY BROTHER...
THERE WAS A REASON I KEPT THIS FROM HIM ALL THOSE YEARS...
SORRY ABOUT THAT...
SORRY ABOUT THE WHOLE 'MAKING YOU FALL OFF A CLIFF' THING AS WELL.
HM.
THEY'VE STOPPED.
WHY HAVE THEY STOPPED HERE?
WE'RE RIGHT ABOVE HER. I CAN HEAR HER VOICE CLEARER THAN EVER.
POP!
LOOK!
WHAT'S HAPPENING TO THEM?

s the trolls began to spring into bloom, a voice echoed up from the ground below them...

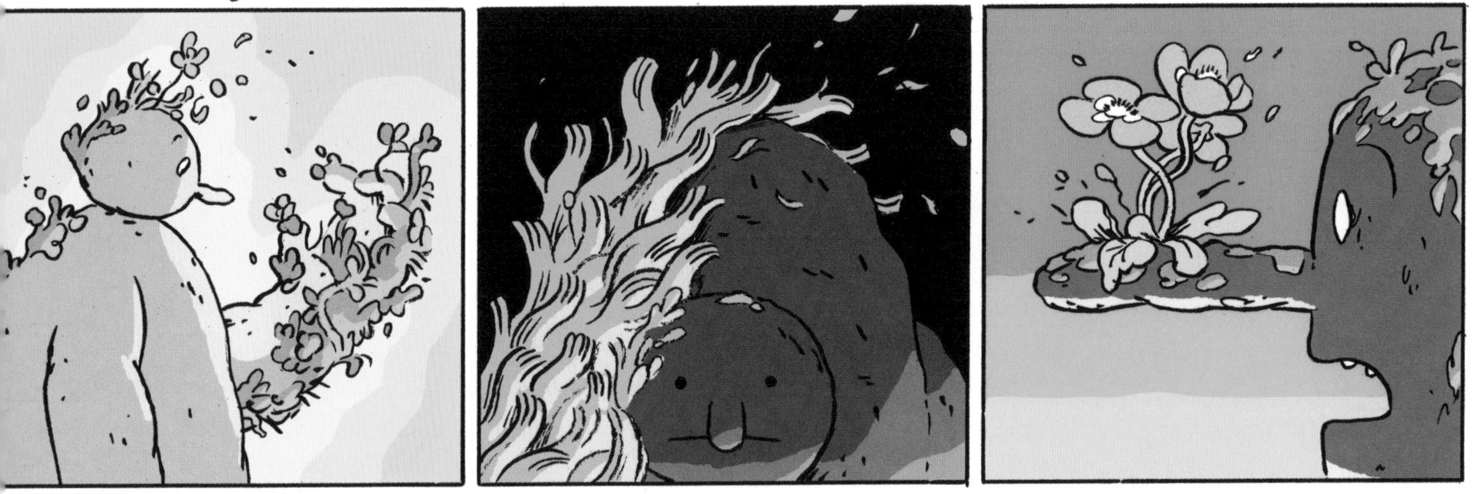

t's hard to accurately translate the troll's language, but her words were along the lines of these:

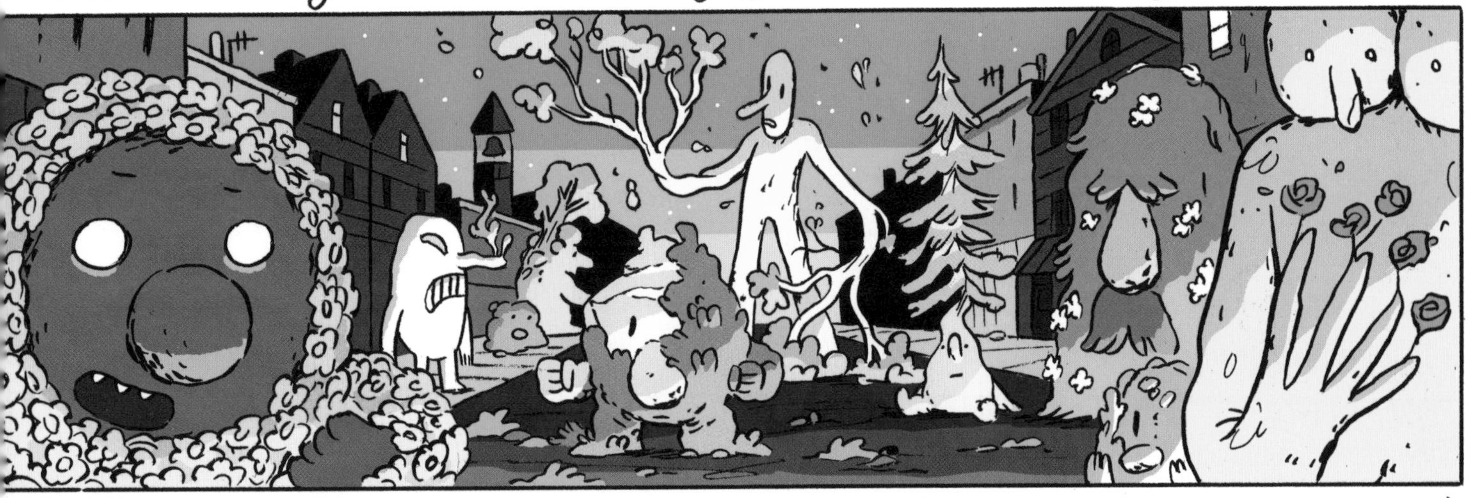

My children, I am proud of you. You may not remember me, but I have never and will never forget you."

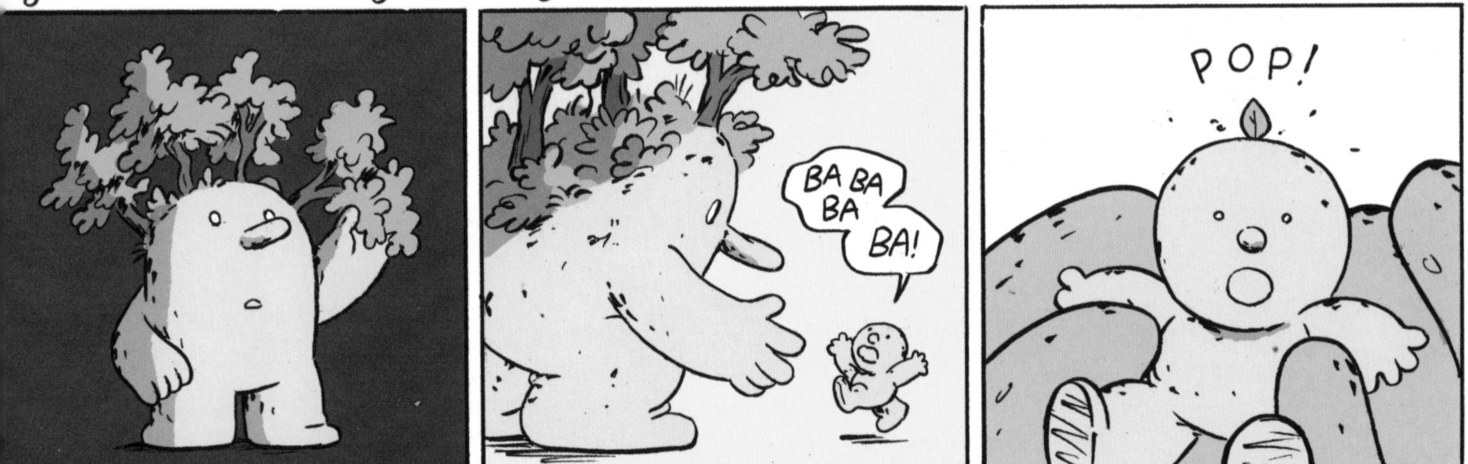
BA BA BA BA!
POP!

"Take care of one another, be strong, be good and know that I am never very far away..."

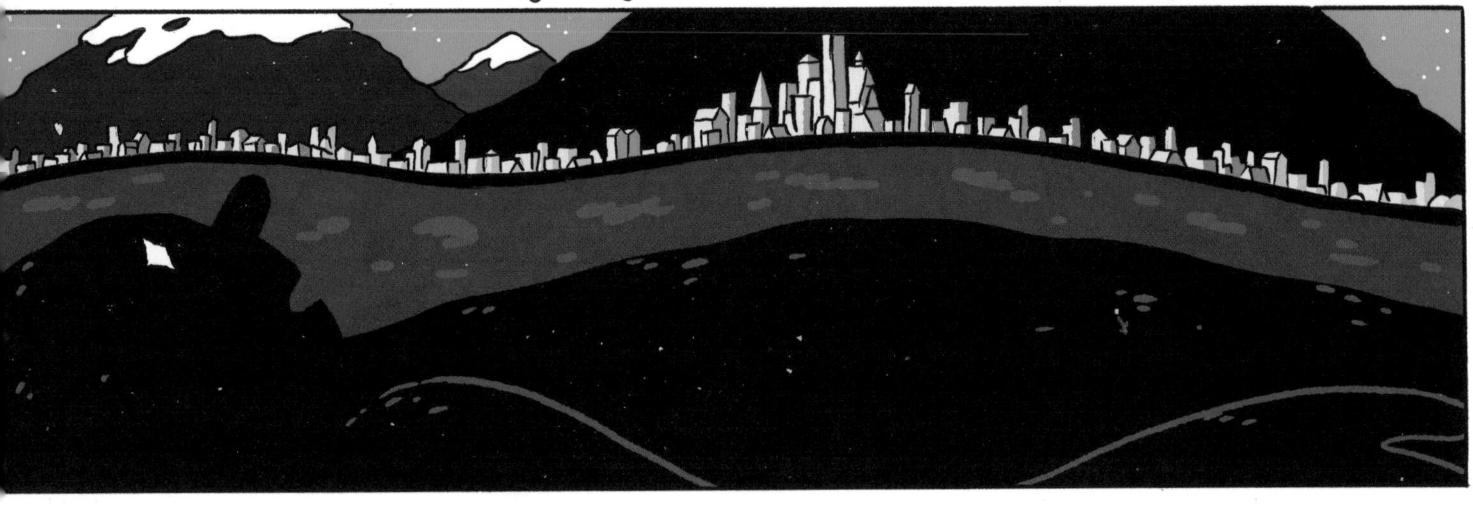

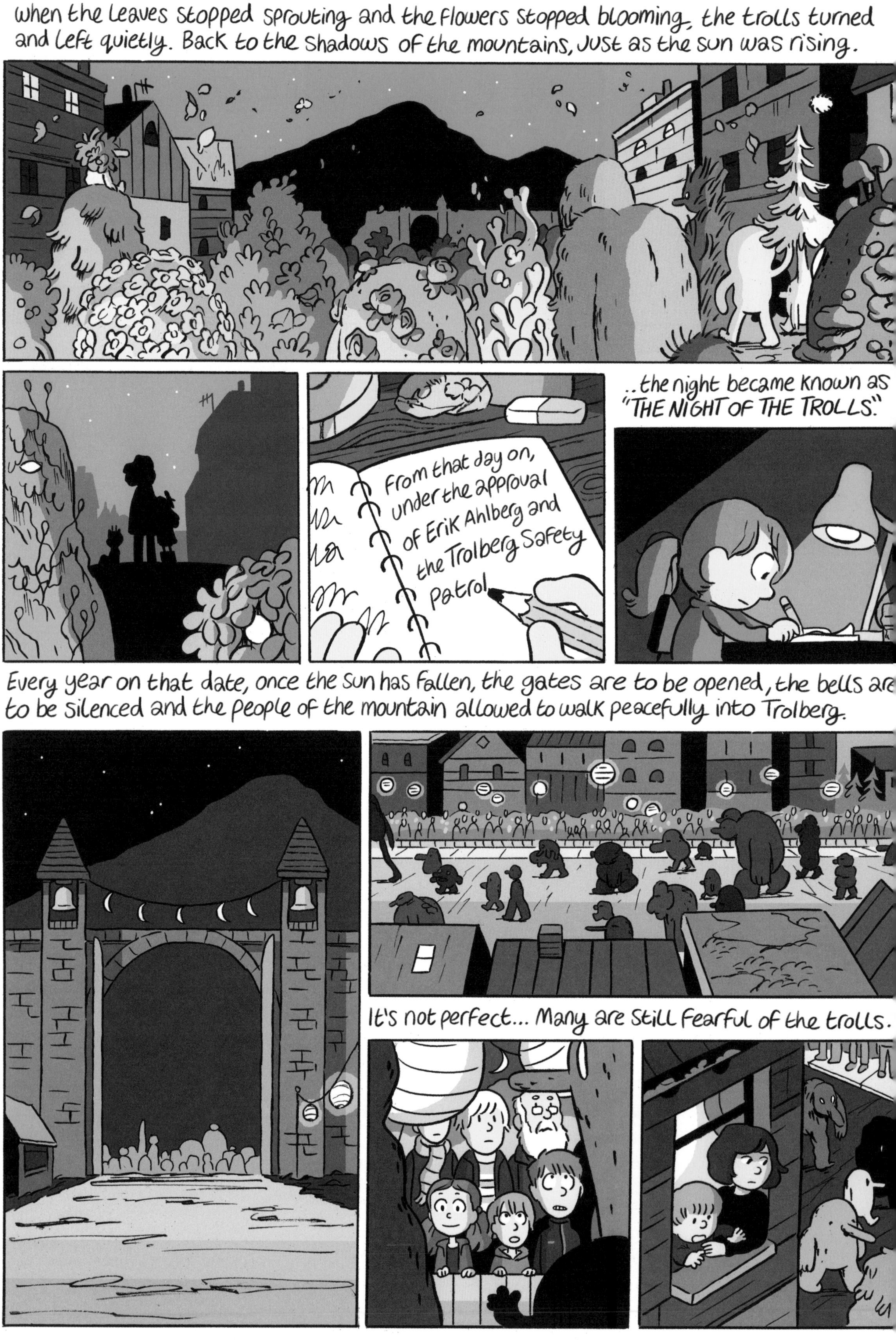
when the leaves stopped sprouting and the flowers stopped blooming, the trolls turned and left quietly. Back to the shadows of the mountains, just as the sun was rising.
From that day on, under the approval of Erik Ahlberg and the Trolberg Safety patrol
...the night became known as "THE NIGHT OF THE TROLLS."
Every year on that date, once the sun has fallen, the gates are to be opened, the bells are to be silenced and the people of the mountain allowed to walk peacefully into Trolberg.
It's not perfect... Many are still fearful of the trolls.

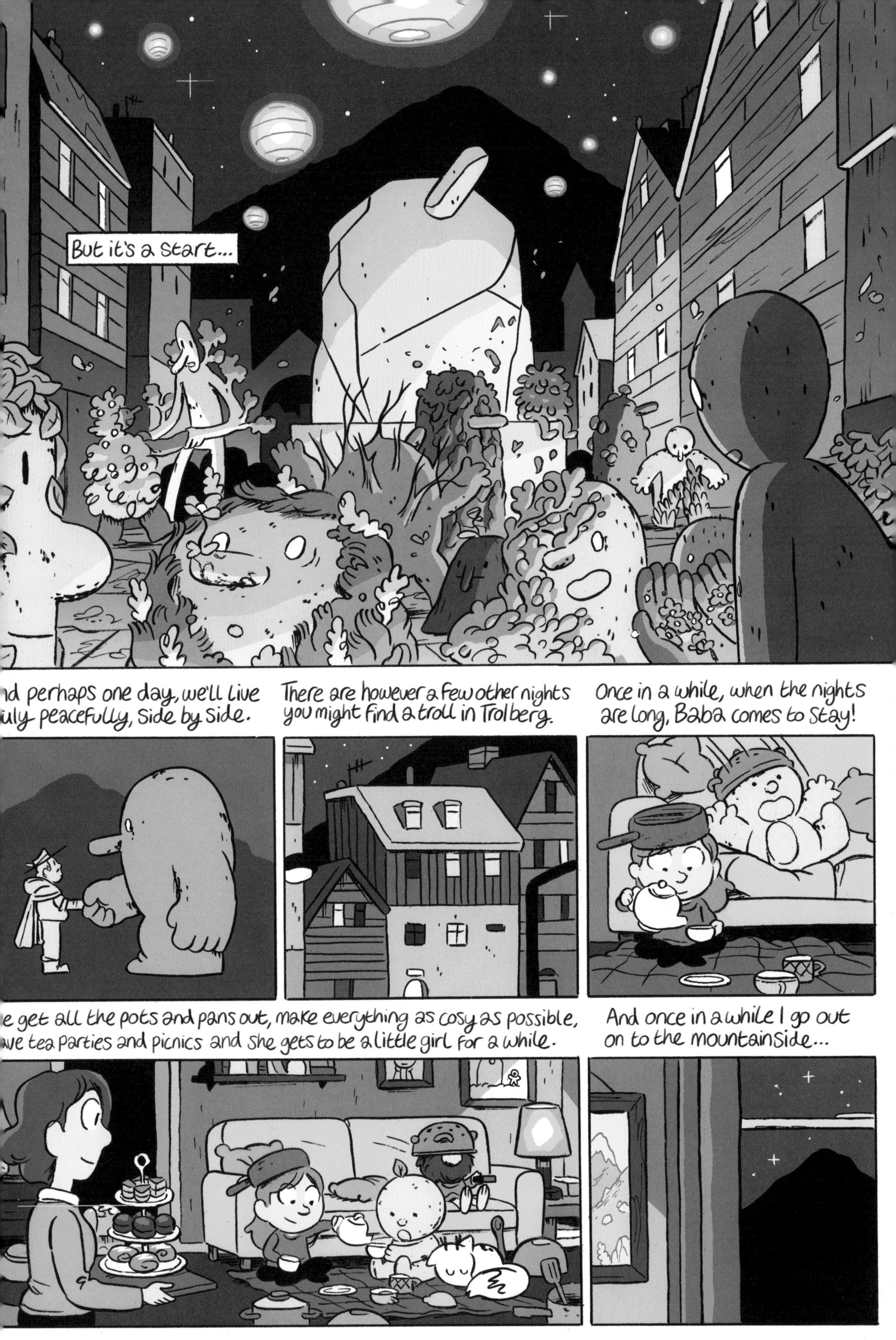
But it's a start...
d perhaps one day, we'll live
uly peacefully, side by side.
There are however a few other nights
you might find a troll in Trolberg.
Once in a while, when the nights
are long, Baba comes to stay!
e get all the pots and pans out, make everything as cosy as possible,
ve tea parties and picnics and she gets to be a little girl for a while.
And once in a while I go out
on to the mountainside...

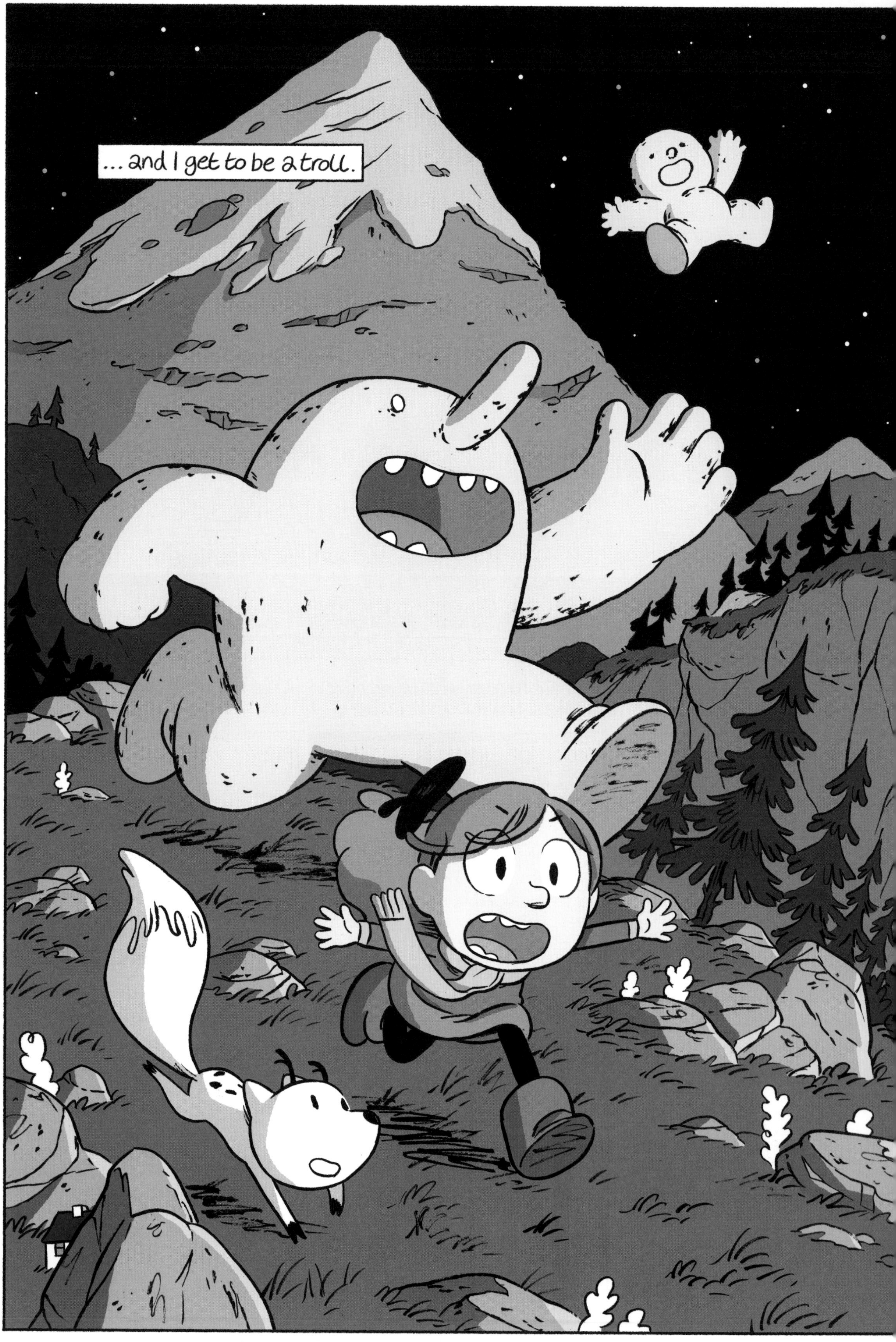
... and I get to be a troll.

Have you read all the Hilda graphic novels?
Make sure you're all caught up with the series so far...

LUKE PEARSON
HILDA AND THE TROLL
FLYING EYE BOOKS
LUKE PEARSON
HILDA AND THE MIDNIGHT GIANT
FLYING EYE BOOKS
LUKE PEARSON
HILDA AND THE BIRD PARADE
FLYING EYE BOOKS
LUKE PEARSON
HILDA AND THE BLACK HOUND
LUKE PEARSON
HILDA AND THE STONE FOREST
FLYING EYE BOOKS

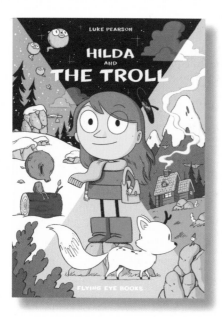

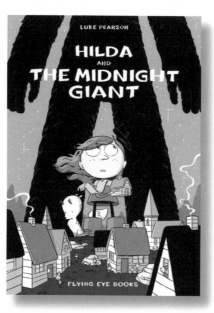

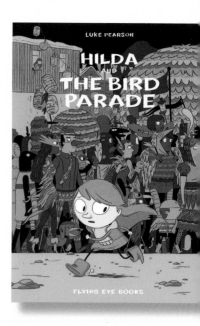

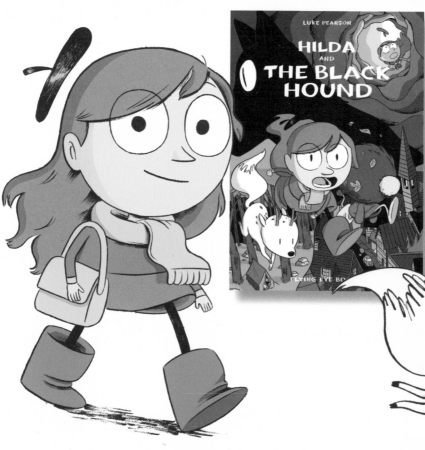

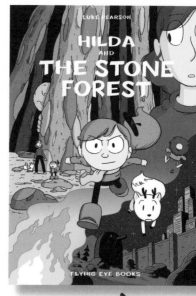